GHOSTS, GHOSTS, GHOSTS

★

OTHER TRIPLE TITLES

Horses, Horses, Horses
Witches, Witches, Witches
Danger, Danger, Danger
Doctors, Doctors, Doctors
Spooks, Spooks, Spooks
Dogs, Dogs, Dogs

GHOSTS
GHOSTS, GHOSTS

Stories of
Spooks and Spirits
Haunts and Hobgoblins, Werewolves
and Will-o'-the-wisps

selected by
PHYLLIS R. FENNER

illustrated by
MANNING de V. LEE

Chatto and Windus
London

Published by
CHATTO AND WINDUS LTD
42 WILLIAM IV STREET
LONDON WC2

First Published 1955
Second Impression 1958
Third Impression 1961
Fourth Impression 1965
Fifth Impression 1967
Sixth Impression 1970
Seventh Impression 1972
Eighth Impression 1975

ISBN 0 7011 0218 7

Printed in Great Britain by
Redwood Burn Limited, Trowbridge & Esher

For
HELEN and FRANK
who literally haunt me
with ideas

ILLUSTRATIONS

CONTENTS

ACKNOWLEDGMENTS

To Walter R. Brooks for *Jimmy Takes Vanishing Lessons*, by Walter R. Brooks. Copyright 1950.

To Houghton Mifflin Company for *Spooks of the Valley* from *Spooks of of the Valley*, by Louis C. Jones. Copyright 1948.

To Franklin Watts, Inc. for *Not Quite Martin* from *This Boy Cody*, by Leon Wilson. Copyright 1950.

To Irving Crump for *Dead Men on Parade*, by Irving Crump. Copyright 1929. Reprinted by permission of the author and *Boys' Life*, published by the Boy Scouts of America.

To Alfred A. Knopf, Inc. for *The House of Ocean Born Mary* from *Ghosts That Still Walk*, by Marion Lowndes. Copyright 1941.

To the Viking Press, Inc. for *Fiddler, Play Fast, Play Faster* from *The Long Christmas*, by Ruth Sawyer. Copyright 1941.

To Harper & Brothers for *The Water Ghost of Harrowby Hall* from *The Water Ghost and Others*, by John Kendrick Bangs.

To Longmans, Green and Co. for *The Golden Pitcher* from *Castles in Spain and Other Enchantments*, by Bertha L. Gunterman. Copyright 1928.

To Roy Publishers a.n. New York for *Prince Godfrey Frees Mountain Dwellers and Little Shepherds from A Savage Werewolf and from Witches* from *Prince Godfrey*, by Halina Gorska. Copyright 1946.

To The Executors of Mrs. Jan Struther Placzek for *Cobbler, Cobbler Mend My Shoe* from *A Pocketful of Pebbles*, by Jan Struther. Copyright 1946.

To Stephen Vincent Benet for *The Devil and Daniel Webster* from *Selected Works of Stephen Vincent Benet*, by Stephen Vincent Benet, published by Rinehart & Company, Inc. Copyright 1936.

To Rupert Sargent Holland for *The Cobra's Hood* from *Yankee Ships in Pirate Waters*, by Rupert Sargent Holland, published by Macrae Smith Co. Copyright 1931.

What's a Ghost?

"It's someone who ain't," said the little boy. "No," said his friend, "It's someone who is but who looks like he ain't." So there you have it, all nice and clear. Now you know what a ghost really is, and you'd recognize him if you met him.

They go by many names: spooks, spirits, phantoms, spectres, ha'nts. There are good ghosts and bad ghosts; lively, mischievous ghosts and oh-so-sad ghosts who walk because they are unhappy creatures, eternally searching for something, or uneasy until something has been put right, like the ghost in this book who wanted his bones all collected in one spot. There are even animal ghosts, pets who come back to their masters, or wild animals who guide people out of trouble like the white stag did the Huns. There are ghost riders heard in the night. A bus once disappeared with all of its passengers, so the story goes, and now, once in awhile in the night, a phantom bus is seen to slide swiftly along the highway.

Empty houses, graveyards and old inns with dire histories are supposed to be haunted. In one such the ghost of an old sea captain with a wooden leg walks each night down the stairs with a clomp, clomp, clomp. Many people swear to hearing him. Ocean-born Mary of whom you'll read in this book has been seen by many, dropping something down the well.

If you feel a prickly sensation at the back of your neck, a slight breeze as of someone passing you on the stairs, it may be just a poor lonely ghost going about his ghostly business.

P. F.

Jimmy Takes Vanishing Lessons

By WALTER R. BROOKS

The school bus picked up Jimmy Crandall every morning at the side road that led up to his aunt's house, and every afternoon it dropped him there again. And so twice a day, on the bus, he passed the entrance to the mysterious road.

It wasn't much of a road any more. It was choked with weeds and blackberry bushes, and the woods on both sides pressed in so closely that the branches met overhead, and it was dark and gloomy even on bright days. The bus driver once pointed it out.

"Folks that go in there after dark," he said, "well, they usually don't ever come out again. There's a haunted house about a quarter of a mile down that road." He paused. "But you ought to know about that, Jimmy. It was your grandfather's house."

Jimmy knew about it, and he knew that it now belonged to his Aunt Mary. But Jimmy's aunt would never talk to him about the house. She said the stories about it were silly nonsense and there were no such things as

This story is from Story Parade *magazine*

ghosts. If all the villagers weren't a lot of superstitious idiots, she would be able to rent the house, and then she would have enough money to buy Jimmy some decent clothes and take him to the movies.

Jimmy thought it was all very well to say that there were no such things as ghosts, but how about the people who had tried to live there? Aunt Mary had rented the house three times, but every family had moved out within a week. They said the things that went on there were just too queer. So nobody would live in it any more.

Jimmy thought about the house a lot. If he could only prove that there wasn't a ghost. . . . And one Saturday when his aunt was in the village, Jimmy took the key to the haunted house from its hook on the kitchen door, and started out.

It had seemed like a fine idea when he had first thought of it—to find out for himself. Even in the silence and damp gloom of the old road it still seemed pretty good. Nothing to be scared of, he told himself. Ghosts aren't around in the daytime. But when he came out in the clearing and looked at those blank, dusty windows, he wasn't so sure.

"Oh, come on!" he told himself. And he squared his shoulders and waded through the long grass to the porch.

Then he stopped again. His feet did not seem to want to go up the steps. It took him nearly five minutes to persuade them to move. But when at last they did, they marched right up and across the porch to the front door, and Jimmy set his teeth hard and put the key in the key-hole. It turned with a squeak. He pushed the door open and went in.

That was probably the bravest thing that Jimmy had ever done. He was in a long dark hall with closed doors on both sides, and on the right the stairs went up. He had left the door open behind him, and the light from it showed him that, except for the hatrack and table and chairs, the hall was empty. And then as he stood there, listening to the bumping of his heart, gradually the light faded, the hall grew darker and darker—as if something huge had come up on the porch behind him and stood there, blocking the doorway. He swung round quickly, but there was nothing there.

He drew a deep breath. It must have been just a cloud passing across the sun. But then the door, all of itself, began to swing shut. And before he could stop it, it closed with a bang. And it was then, as he was pulling frantically at the handle to get out, that Jimmy saw the ghost.

It behaved just as you would expect a ghost to behave. It was a tall, dim, white figure, and it came gliding slowly down the stairs towards him. Jimmy gave a yell, yanked the door open, and tore down the steps.

He didn't stop until he was well down the road. Then he had to get his breath. He sat down on a log. "Boy!" he said. "I've seen a ghost! Golly, was that awful!" Then after a minute, he thought, "What was so awful about it? He was trying to scare me, like that smart aleck who was always jumping out from behind things. Pretty silly business for a grown-up ghost to be doing."

It always makes you mad when someone deliberately tries to scare you. And as Jimmy got over his fright, he began to get angry. And pretty soon he got up and started back. "I must get that key, anyway," he thought, for he had left it in the door.

This time he approached very quietly. He thought he'd just lock the door and go home. But as he tiptoed up the steps he saw it was still open; and as he reached out cautiously for the key, he heard a faint sound. He drew back and peeked around the door jamb, and there was the ghost.

The ghost was going back upstairs, but he wasn't gliding now, he was doing a sort of dance, and every other step he would bend double and shake with laughter. His thin cackle was the sound Jimmy had heard. Evidently he was enjoying the joke he had played. That made Jimmy madder than ever. He stuck his head farther around the door jamb and yelled "Boo!" at the top of his lungs. The ghost gave a thin shriek and leaped two feet in the air, then collapsed on the stairs.

As soon as Jimmy saw he could scare the ghost even worse than the ghost could scare him, he wasn't afraid any more, and he came right into the hall. The ghost was hanging on to the bannisters and panting. "Oh, my goodness!" he gasped. "Oh, my gracious! Boy, you can't *do* that to me!"

"I did it, didn't I?" said Jimmy. "Now we're even."

would be in terrible trouble."

So they argued about it. The ghost said if Jimmy wanted money he could learn to vanish; then he could join a circus and get a big salary. Jimmy said he didn't want to be in a circus; he wanted to go to college and learn to be a doctor. He was very firm. And the ghost began to cry. "But this is my *home,* boy," he said. "Thirty years I've lived here and no trouble to anybody, and now you want to throw me out into the cold world! And for what? A little money! That's pretty heartless." And he sobbed, trying to make Jimmy feel cruel.

Jimmy didn't feel cruel at all, for the ghost had certainly driven plenty of other people out into the cold world. But he didn't really think it would do much good for him to tell anybody that he had scared the ghost. Nobody would believe him, and how could he prove it? So after a minute he said, "Well, all right. You teach me to vanish and I won't tell." They settled it that way.

Jimmy didn't say anything to his aunt about what he'd done. But every Saturday he went to the haunted house for his vanishing lesson. It is really quite easy when you know how, and in a couple of weeks he could flicker, and in six weeks the ghost gave him an examination and he got a B plus, which is very good for a human. So he thanked the ghost and shook hands with him and said, "Well, good-by now. You'll hear from me."

18

A dim white figure came gliding down the stairs . . .

"Nothing of the kind," said the ghost crossly. "You seem pretty stupid, even for a boy. Ghosts are supposed to scare people. People aren't supposed to scare ghosts." He got up slowly and glided down and sat on the bottom step. "But look here, boy; this could be pretty serious for me if people got to know about it."

"You mean you don't want me to tell anybody about it?" Jimmy asked.

"Suppose we make a deal," the ghost said. "You keep still about this, and in return I'll—well, let's see; how would you like to know how to vanish?"

"Oh, that would be swell!" Jimmy exclaimed. "But —can you vanish?"

"Sure," said the ghost, and he did. All at once he just wasn't there. Jimmy was alone in the hall.

But his voice went right on. "It would be pretty handy, wouldn't it?" he said persuasively. "You could get into the movies free whenever you wanted to, and if your aunt called you to do something—when you were in the yard, say—well, she wouldn't be able to find you."

"I don't mind helping Aunt Mary," Jimmy said.

"H'm. High-minded, eh?" said the ghost. "Well, then—"

"I wish you'd please reappear," Jimmy interrupted. "It makes me feel funny to talk to somebody who isn't there."

"Sorry, I forgot," said the ghost, and there he was again, sitting on the bottom step. Jimmy could see the

step, dimly, right through him. "Good trick, eh? \[...] if you don't like vanishing, maybe I could teach \[...] to seep through keyholes. Like this." He floated \[...] to the door and went right through the keyhole, the \[...] water goes down the drain. Then he came back the s\[...] way.

"That's useful, too," he said. "Getting into loc\[...] rooms and so on. You can go anywhere the wind c\[...]

"No," said Jimmy. "There's only one thing you \[...] do to get me to promise not to tell about scaring y\[...] Go live somewhere else. There's Miller's, up the ro\[...] Nobody lives there any more."

"That old shack!" said the ghost, with a nasty lau\[...] "Doors and windows half off, roof leaky—no than\[...] What do you think it's like in a storm, windows bar\[...] ing, rain dripping on you—I guess not! Peace and qui\[...] that's really what a ghost wants out of life."

"Well, I don't think it's very fair," Jimmy said, "f\[...] you to live in a house that doesn't belong to you a\[...] keep my aunt from renting it."

"Pooh!" said the ghost. "I'm not stopping her fro\[...] renting it. I don't take up any room, and it's not m\[...] fault if people get scared and leave."

"It certainly is!" Jimmy said angrily. "You don\[...] play fair and I'm not going to make any bargain wit\[...] you. I'm going to tell everybody how I scared you."

"Oh, you mustn't do that!" The ghost seemed qui\[...] disturbed and he vanished and reappeared rapidly sev\[...] eral times. "If that got out, every ghost in the countr\[...]

"What do you mean by that?" said the ghost suspiciously. But Jimmy just laughed and ran off home.

That night at supper Jimmy's aunt said, "Well, what have you been doing today?"

"I've been learning to vanish."

His aunt smiled and said, "That must be fun."

"Honestly," said Jimmy. "The ghost up at grandfather's taught me."

"I don't think that's very funny," said his aunt. "And will you please not—why, where are you?" she demanded, for he had vanished.

"Here, Aunt Mary," he said as he reappeared.

"Merciful heavens!" she exclaimed, and she pushed back her chair and rubbed her eyes hard. Then she looked at him again.

Well, it took a lot of explaining and he had to do it twice more before he could persuade her that he really could vanish. She was pretty upset. But at last she calmed down and they had a long talk. Jimmy kept his word and didn't tell her that he had scared the ghost, but he said he had a plan, and at last, though very reluctantly, she agreed to help him.

So the next day she went up to the old house and started to work. She opened the windows and swept and dusted and aired the bedding, and made as much noise as possible. This disturbed the ghost, and pretty soon he came floating into the room where she was sweeping. She was scared all right. She gave a yell and threw the broom at him. As the broom went right through him and he came nearer, waving his arms and groaning, she shrank back.

And Jimmy, who had been standing there invisible all the time, suddenly appeared and jumped at the ghost with a "Boo!" And the ghost fell over in a dead faint.

As soon as Jimmy's aunt saw that, she wasn't frightened any more. She found some smelling salts and held them under the ghost's nose, and when he came to she tried to help him into a chair. Of course she couldn't help him much because her hands went right through him. But at last he sat up and said reproachfully to Jimmy, "You broke your word!"

"I promised not to tell about scaring you," said the boy, "but I didn't promise not to scare you again."

And his aunt said, "You really are a ghost, aren't you? I thought you were just stories people made up. Well, excuse me, but I must get on with my work." And she began sweeping and banging around with her broom harder than ever.

The ghost put his hands to his head. "All this noise," he said. "Couldn't you work more quietly, ma'am?"

"Whose house is this, anyway?" she demanded. "If you don't like it, why don't you move out?"

The ghost sneezed violently several times. "Excuse me," he said. "You're raising so much dust. Where's that boy?" he asked suddenly. For Jimmy had vanished again.

"I'm sure I don't know," she replied. "Probably getting ready to scare you again."

"You ought to have better control of him," said the ghost severely. "If he was my boy, I'd take a hairbrush to him."

"You have my permission," she said, and she reached right through the ghost and pulled the chair cushion out from under him and began banging the dust out of it. "What's more," she went on, as he got up and glided wearily to another chair, "Jimmy and I are going to sleep here nights from now on, and I don't think it would be very smart of you to try any tricks."

"Ha, ha," said the ghost nastily. "He who laughs last—"

"Ha, ha, yourself," said Jimmy's voice from close behind him. "And that's me, laughing last."

The ghost muttered and vanished.

Jimmy's aunt put cotton in her ears and slept that night in the best bedroom with the light lit. The ghost screamed for a while down in the cellar, but nothing happened, so he came upstairs. He thought he would appear to her as two glaring, fiery eyes, which was one of his best tricks, but first he wanted to be sure where Jimmy was. But he couldn't find him. He hunted all over the house, and though he was invisible himself, he got more and more nervous. He kept imagining that at any moment Jimmy might jump out at him from some dark corner and scare him into fits. Finally he got so jittery that he went back to the cellar and hid in the coal bin all night.

The following days were just as bad for the ghost.

Several times he tried to scare Jimmy's aunt while she was working, but she didn't scare worth a cent, and twice Jimmy managed to sneak up on him and appear suddenly with a loud yell, frightening him dreadfully. He was, I suppose, rather timid even for a ghost. He began to look quite haggard. He had several long arguments with Jimmy's aunt, in which he wept and appealed to her sympathy, but she was firm. If he wanted to live there he would have to pay rent, just like anybody else. There was the abandoned Miller farm two miles up the road. Why didn't he move there?

When the house was all in apple-pie order, Jimmy's aunt went down to the village to see a Mr. and Mrs. Whistler, who were living at the hotel because they couldn't find a house to move into. She told them about the old house, but they said, "No, thank you. We've heard about that house. It's haunted. I'll bet," they said, "*you* wouldn't dare spend a night there."

She told them that she had spent the last week there, but they evidently didn't believe her. So she said, "You know my nephew, Jimmy. He's twelve years old. I am so sure that the house is not haunted that, if you want to rent it, I will let Jimmy stay there with you every night until you are sure everything is all right."

"Ha!" said Mr. Whistler. "The boy won't do it. He's got more sense."

So they sent for Jimmy. "Why, I've spent the last week there," he said. "Sure. I'd just as soon."

But the Whistlers still refused.

22

So Jimmy's aunt went around and told a lot of the village people about their talk, and everybody made so much fun of the Whistlers for being afraid, when a twelve-year-old boy wasn't, that they were ashamed, and said they would rent it. So they moved in. Jimmy stayed there for a week, but he saw nothing of the ghost. And then one day one of the boys in his grade told him that somebody had seen a ghost up at the Miller farm. So Jimmy knew the ghost had taken his aunt's advice.

A day or two later he walked up to the Miller farm. There was no front door and he walked right in. There was some groaning and thumping upstairs, and then after a minute the ghost came floating down.

"Oh, it's you!" he said. "Goodness sakes, boy, can't you leave me in peace?"

Jimmy said he'd just come up to see how he was getting along.

"Getting along fine," said the ghost. "From my point of view it's a very desirable property. Peaceful. Quiet. Nobody playing silly tricks."

"Well," said Jimmy, "I won't bother you if you don't bother the Whistlers. But if you come back there—"

"Don't worry," said the ghost.

So with the rent money, Jimmy and his aunt had a much easier life. They went to the movies sometimes twice a week, and Jimmy had all new clothes, and on Thanksgiving, for the first time in his life, Jimmy had a turkey. Once a week he would go up to the Miller farm to see the ghost and they got to be very good

23

friends. The ghost even came down to the Thanksgiving dinner, though of course he couldn't eat much. He seemed to enjoy the warmth of the house and he was in very good humor. He taught Jimmy several more tricks. The best one was how to glare with fiery eyes, which was useful later on when Jimmy became a doctor and had to look down people's throats to see if their tonsils ought to come out. He was really a pretty good fellow as ghosts go, and Jimmy's aunt got quite fond of him herself. When the real winter weather began, she even used to worry about him a lot, because of course there was no heat in the Miller place and the doors and windows didn't amount to much and there was hardly any roof. The ghost tried to explain to her that heat and cold didn't bother ghosts at all.

"Maybe not," she said, "but just the same, it can't be very pleasant." And when he accepted their invitation for Christmas dinner she knitted some red woolen slippers, and he was so pleased that he broke down and cried. And that made Jimmy's aunt so happy, *she* broke down and cried.

Jimmy didn't cry, but he said, "Aunt Mary, don't you think it would be nice if the ghost came down and lived with us this winter?"

"I would feel very much better about him if he did," she said.

So he stayed with them that winter, and then he just stayed on, and it must have been a peaceful place for the last I heard he was still there.

24

Spooks of the Valley

By LOUIS C. JONES

The boys were working intently on the tail assembly of the model transport plane. Joe was holding the small piece of balsa wood neatly in place while Pete carefully spread the glue along the crevice. It was well after bedtime, for Pete's folks, when they went out, had told the boys to go upstairs at eight-thirty, and now the clock was striking nine. But the problem of the tail was a tough one and could hardly be left for tomorrow. Besides, Joe didn't come to spend the night very often. When they heard the first step on the top stair they hardly noticed it. At the second step Pete spoke up sharply, but without raising his eyes from their task.

"Sis, you get on back to bed. You know what Mom told you. You're gonna get in trouble."

The footsteps kept coming slowly down the stairs just as he rather expected they would, young sisters being what they are. It wasn't the weight on the steps that made him turn, for that was light enough, but Sister never came down a pair of stairs slowly in her life. And

This story is from Spooks of the Valley *by Louis C. Jones*

25

if it wasn't Carol, who was it? This took a few seconds, especially since Pete's mind really wasn't on the stairs but on the model. It wasn't until Joe said, "Okay now," and put the tube of glue down, that Pete turned around.

Never before had he seen the man who stood there —tall and gaunt, with tanned, knotty hands and a weary stoop to his shoulders. His clothes were ragged and strangely out of date. Pete wasn't scared, just surprised. You couldn't really be scared of a face like this man's. It was an interesting face, with kind, sad lines around the mouth and the gray eyes. It looked like a face that had seen a lot of things, and the expression of the eyes made you ponder. Pete was still gaping when Joe spoke.

"Well, hello, George! So you really came up, did you?"

"Yeah," the man said, "I figured you two would be alone tonight so I kind of hung around outside until Pete's folks went away. Then I just wandered in and looked around until I found you."

"Who is this guy?" Pete asked, still surprised not to see his sister.

"This is George, Pete. I told you about George. I told you all about him on the bus the other day."

"You mean," said Pete, "that you weren't kidding? I thought you made all that up."

"Pete, you know I never make things up. I'm not always having crazy ideas like you. George, this is Pete."

"Pete, I'm glad to meet you. I'm mighty glad to meet

you, 'cause I think you can help me," said George in a hopeful voice.

"Gee, I'd like to help you, George," said Pete. "That is—I guess I would. Are you really—I mean, is it like Joe told me? Aren't you—"

"Well, now, Pete, I don't know. I don't know just what Joe told you. If he told you how I used to peddle tin all through this section, and how this was the last farm I ever stopped at, and how I'm needing your help now—I guess he told you right. You see, Pete, the way it is, I can't rest. I got this thing on my mind all the time, and that way you don't get any rest. People ought not to do things like that, and it was a long time ago, of course, and somebody who lives here now has got to make it right. I tried to get to your old man, and I tried to get to your mom, but they couldn't hear me and they couldn't see me. I figured maybe you were the only one I could talk to."

"Well, gee, George, I guess we can help you if it isn't too hard to do. Do we have to do it tonight?"

"Well," said George, "it would be kind of nice if you could. This business is sort of delicate, but there's a good moon out, and though I don't want to get you in trouble, it will be quite a spell before your folks get back."

He seemed so earnest and hopeful about it that the boys felt they really had to help.

"How do we start?" asked Joe.

"All you got to do, boys, is this. You go out to that

big woodpile—the old woodpile in the back of the barn—"

"We haven't touched that woodpile since we moved here four years ago," broke in Pete. "Pop cut down so many trees and sawed 'em up for firewood that we just haven't had to use that wood out behind the barn."

"I know that, son," said George, "and nobody else has touched that woodpile. Some of that wood's been there ten years, and before that they kept putting fresh wood on every winter, so that nobody's been down to the bottom of that pile since 1853. But all I want you boys to do is go down to the far end of that pile and tear it to pieces. Get right down to the ground and then start digging until you come to the place where my tin is buried. Won't be much now—just a few pieces of rust —but then you'll know you're in the right spot and you keep digging down below that. Then you come to the important thing. . . ."

Pete was listening intently to every word George said, and then suddenly he realized that something weird and wonderful was happening. George was disappearing. It was not that he was going away—it's just that when he finished the sentence, he wasn't there. First there had been three of them and now there were only two.

"Whillikers!" said Pete, "I'd somehow forgotten all about his being dead."

Pete ran upstairs and looked in to see if his brother and sister were asleep. They certainly were, all right. Carol was snoring happily to herself and Davie was hugging his little old bear for dear life. Then Pete got some mittens and a couple of sweaters, because the October air was cold. Both boys walked out the back door and down behind the barn where the full moon shone cold and clear on the old woodpile, six feet high and four cord wide.

The wood was dry and light, and they started at the top and threw it off the cord so it fell every which way in the grass. After a little bit Joe was puffing and Pete had stopped to sit down and rest himself.

"This isn't easy!" Pete said slowly.

"But we gotta do it. I promised George that first night I met him."

"How'd you get mixed up in this, Joe?"

"It was like I told you—that calf Pa gave me got her foot caught in a stanchion. I heard her bellowing and went down to the barn along about nine o'clock to get it loose. Coming back, I saw lights in the old Staats house. I knew the Staatses weren't there, and down the little road between our house and theirs I saw George pacing up and down. 'Course I didn't know he was a —I mean, I thought he was just a man. I didn't see any reason to be scared of him, so I says 'Hello' and he says 'Hello, you're Joe, aren't you?' And I says, 'Yep, I'm Joe. I never saw you around before.' So he says, 'No, but I been watching you. Sometimes I see you down here and sometimes I see you visitin' up to your friend Pete's.' So I says, 'Do you know Pete?' And he says,

'Nope, but I wish I did. He's about the only one could really help me.' 'What's the matter?' I says to him, and he comes back with 'What I got, the trouble with me, is hard to say. I'm not like you. I been dead, you know, 'most a hundred years.' Well, when he said it like that, Pete, I could have jumped. We see 'em around, of course. Especially at night around the Staats place where they like to come—they have parties down there sometimes. But I never talked to one, 'specially not about being a ghost. You might say he was just matter of fact about it. Like I'd say, 'I'm a boy.' That's the way he said it."

Pete was quiet for a minute. Then he said, "I think I would have been scared."

"You weren't scared tonight when George came in. The dead seem so natural, don't they?"

There was a long silence then. Somewhere a lone bird chirped just a little. Mr. Ostrander's cow complained in the next field. It was awful quiet. After a bit the boys got up and began pulling down the pile again. They were halfway done now. Their hands were getting tired and they were slowing down. After a while they took another spell of sitting, and Pete said, "When did he tell you, exactly, about this?"

"It was that same night after I had gone to bed. George came into the room and sat down and told me. It seems that the year this all happened, he was carrying around all the money he had saved up for five years. He was gonna open a little store down in Hudson or

Catskill or someplace. He didn't know anybody to take
care of the money for him and he didn't trust banks, so
he had it all wadded up in big bills in his pants' pocket.
It came along toward winter and he had pretty well sold
out everything he had. When he started out he had had
a horse and cart piled up with tin—pots, pans, and stuff.
He was down to four or five pans, and the week before
he had had a chance to sell his horse and cart for a good
price. He wasn't going to need them when he opened
up his store so he grabbed the chance and sold out.

"Well, he came to your house along about dusk one
night and some new folks had bought the place. There
was a man and a woman with the meanest hired man he
had ever seen in his life—a great burly fellow with
hairy arms, and his teeth stuck out of the corners like a
dog. George asked them could he stay there that night.
All he wanted was a place to lay his blanket. They said
he could sleep on the floor up in the hired man's room."

"That must be my room now, isn't it?" asked Pete,
trying to get a word in edgewise.

"That's the way I figure it. Anyway, this hired man
didn't like the idea, was mighty crabby about it.

"When they were getting undressed George suddenly
sneezed and he pulled his handkerchief out and this big
wad of bills came with it. The fellow saw the bills and
didn't say much, but after George had got to sleep he
had this dream about not being able to breathe. Just as
he was waking up, he opened his eyes, and the moonlight was coming right on the face of this great big fel-

low who was choking the very life out of him. Well, sir, he was dead before he knew it.

"Then he stayed around while the hired man picked up his body and very carefully came down those back stairs from your bedroom, down through the kitchen, out in back where this woodpile is—right here where we're sitting. And George says first he took the wood down just like we've done now. Then he dug a grave under where the woodpile had been, putting the dirt into bushel baskets. Then he buried George and put the tin that was left on top, covered it over with dirt and piled up the wood again the way it had been. Then he took the dirt that was left and spread it all over the garden. The next morning he just told the folks that the tin man had left at the crack of dawn."

Maybe it was the cold, maybe it was a stray owl that was hooting out in the pine trees, maybe it was the funny shadows that passed over the moon—but Pete sat on the woodpile shivering.

"Look, Joe, what do you say we do this some other time? I'm not so sure I want to get mixed up in this."

"You wouldn't let me down now, would you?" came a third voice from the darkness. And there was George, standing there looking at him, sad as he could be.

"Pete, my boy, you don't know what it is to have your body buried off in a forsaken spot like the bottom of a woodpile. A man likes to feel he's buried with people. You don't have to have a fancy monument, but the place for a dead man is in a cemetery, and I can't rest like a man ought to until my bones are taken out of this place and put where they belong."

"What about this hired man, George?" Pete's voice was small and sort of sick sounding.

"Oh, him!" George answered. "It didn't take me long to handle him. Two days after he'd killed me, he ran away from here, and I followed him. He went out and walked along the railroad track. About two miles from here, just beyond Van Hoesen, a train came pounding down the line and he stepped off the track, but not quite far enough. I gave him a little shove and that was the end of him. It's a bad thing to have a dead man mad at you. It's a worse thing to steal a dead man's money— 'specially if it's every cent he's saved for six hard years. I tell you, Pete, I never hurt a single soul as long as I was alive, but he was a bummer and I fixed him in my own time."

Pete's worry wasn't quite caught up.

"He isn't still around by any chance?" he asked apprehensively.

"I never saw him," said George. "He never comes down with the others to the Staats place when we have our meetings. No, I never saw him again."

After a pause, he said, "Now what do you say, boys —let's get this done. There isn't much time, you know, before your folks get back."

They worked hard for a few minutes and then another few and before they knew it, sure enough, they were down to the bare ground. Pete disappeared and came back with a spade and a shovel—and while George watched, they dug.

Now this was really hard work and they began to sweat and pant. Just as it seemed an endless job, there was a scraping noise and something more than stone was in the dirt. When they picked it up, it was the handle of a skillet. George remembered it.

"A first-rate piece of merchandise." That's what he said of it. But now there was just a handle—the rest had rusted away. But there were other pieces of metal and the boys kept digging.

"Take it easy now. I think you're getting close," George cautioned. And, sure enough, pretty soon a bone like the upper part of a man's arm lay in the dirt. Pete got a bushel basket and put it in very gently. Joe kept digging and soon they found another. And another. Finally the skull—full of dirt and worms, but clean as it could be once you knocked the soil away. As George watched them carefully putting each piece in the basket, he spoke softly:

"You're very kind to me, boys. Very thoughtful young men you are."

Pretty soon Joe asked him, "Have we got it all there now? Seems like we've picked a couple of hundred bones out of the dirt. They're hard to see, you know, even in this moonlight."

"I think there's a hand missing, boys. It feels to me that way. I don't feel you've got my other hand yet."

"Do you have any idea where it would be?" Joe asked.

"Try right there," said George and pointed.

They dug a little more and pretty soon they found the bones as though they had been all clenched together and the boys picked them up in a couple of handfuls. They took the basket and hid it in the haymow in the barn and then came back to fill the hole in just as fast as they could move. Then they piled up the wood again as best they could. Fortunately, that was a part of the farm where almost no one ever came, so its chance of being seen was pretty small. The midnight express went screaming down the B. & A. tracks a mile away about the time the boys had piled the last stick in place.

The past half hour Pete had been getting nervous because he knew that it was almost time for his folks to be coming home and if he weren't in bed asleep, they'd make an awful squawk. And if they knew what he had been up to, there was no telling what would happen. Every time a car light came up the road he would look over his shoulder at it.

"What's the matter, Pete?" George asked. "You ain't still worrying about that hired man, are you?"

"No, I was more worried about my old man than your hired man. It's about time they're comin' home."

"Oh, them," said George, "don't worry about them. I had one of my friends in town stick a nail in your father's tire, just so he wouldn't hurry home too fast. I don't think he'll be here for a spell yet. And, boys, I

Finally they unearthed the skull . . .

want to say how grateful I am to you, but there's one other little matter. Where are you going to rebury me?"

"Well," said Joe, "I thought we'd take you down to that old burying ground outside the Staats place. It would be near the house down there and handy for your parties."

"That's fine," said George, "that's fine. Now, when?" There was persistence in his tone.

"Well," said Pete, "I'm going down to Joe's to spend Saturday night and if you wouldn't mind my putting the bones in a bag, I could take them down on my bike when I go. Then we could fix it up for you sometime over the weekend."

"Boys, that's just fine. That's just fine. Down there I'll be real happy. If there's anything I can ever do for you, you let me know."

"It's okay," said Joe, "we're glad to help you out."

"Would you—sometime—" broke off Pete, not knowing how to go on.

"What, son? Anything at all."

"Saturday, mebbe, would you tell us more about—about being dead? And about some of the ghosts—the other ghosts, I mean."

"Why not? I'll tell you all I know—and what I don't know ain't worth knowin'." And for the first time George grinned at them. "You bury me the way I ought to be, and then Saturday we'll get together. How's that?" They were about to answer him, but George had disappeared once more.

Right after breakfast on Saturday Pete fed the chickens and before his mother quite realized it, he was off on his bike for Joe's house. In the basket on his handle bars was a grain bag, neatly folded. It made an irregular package but it weighed so little that he barely realized it was there. Best of all, he had been able to hide it up by the trees at the north end of his farm the night before, so that in the morning he could pick it up without the endless questions that grown-ups are forever asking a boy.

Pete lived two miles or more back from the Hudson, high above the river. He pedaled along rapidly, finally coming to the airport road which dropped down to the river road, past Citizen Genet's old house. As he swung down the hill, bracing himself against the pull of the brakes, he caught the long view of the river with Albany to the right, its hillside towers against the sky, then far to the left the Castleton bridge carrying the freight trains over the cut-off. When he reached the river road he turned left for a mile, then took a side road leading to the river.

Joe lived on an island, separated from the mainland by a longish bridge. Before the river was deepened it was more of an island, but even now during the spring floods sometimes they were cut off from the mainland. As Pete pumped his bike up over the New York Central tracks he could see the farm buildings ahead of him, the ancient barns and the farmhouse made over and modernized but really the same house that had been there for nearly two centuries.

"Hi, Joeyeeee." It made a crazy sound as Pete called it.

But back from the barn came "Hiyi, Pete." And Joe came running.

Five minutes later the two boys were walking rapidly down the little grass-covered wagon track that led to the south end of the island and the old Staats house with its aged cemetery. Each carried a shovel over his shoulder and the bag of bones between them, not because it was heavy, but to share the responsibility.

"George was here last night," said Joe casually.

"Yeah?"

"He told me just where he wants them buried. Over near old Jakob Staats in the far corner. Says the old man was a good customer of his and a good friend. And besides, no one will notice a new grave there."

By now they had come to the gateway of the little family burying ground with its headstones that told the story of a family that are said to have come to the Hudson Valley sometime before 1640 and had always lived on that land. The boys found Jakob's grave off in its far corner, just as George had told Joe they would, and they began to dig. It was easy going, for the soil was sandy.

"How deep do you think we ought to go?" Pete asked when they were down a couple of feet.

"Six feet is the customary depth," said a voice that made them jump halfway out of their skins.

"Holy Moses, George! I wish you wouldn't scare us so," scolded Joe.

"I thought you had to wait till night, George. Can you come around any—Hey, George, where are you?" Pete was bewildered, for, close as the voice was, there was no George to be seen.

"Pete, my friend," the old man said, "your notions about us dead are way out of date. Any time of day or night, that's us. Sometimes we 'show' and sometimes we don't; that's up to us. Look!"

And sure enough, after a second or two there he was, as real as a tree. Then he roared with laughter, slapping his thigh, as he saw the look on the boys' faces. "There are a lot of silly notions going around about us. Chain rattling, for instance. Almost nobody, that is, no *dead* body, rattles chains, that I know of. And water! They tell you we can't cross water. Fiddle-faddle! How would the whole bunch of us get to an *island* for our meetings and parties, down here at the Staats house, if we couldn't cross water? As a matter of fact, we can do almost anything we could when we were alive. More things, really. Couldn't disappear when I was alive." And with that he wasn't there any more, just the sound of his laugh as the boys stared at the air where he had been.

"George is feeling a lot more cheerful, isn't he?" Pete observed.

"Told me he felt like a new spirit since we dug him up," Joe said. "He's much more fun than he was."

They dug for a spell, thinking over what they had heard, thinking, too, about the fact that George was there by them, watching. They figured the hole didn't have to be very long or wide. First one would get down and work awhile, then the other. They did a lot of resting, but not even Joe was talking much. The deeper they went, the harder going it was. When Pete was waist-deep he said, "George, that isn't six feet, but how about it? Don't you think that's deep enough?"

"We-ell, lads, each of you do six more shovelfuls and we'll call it a day. But if we don't get it right now, I'll have trouble later. Get it right and I can rest easy till Judgment Day."

"Won't we be seeing you any more after this, George?"

"Today and tonight. Then I'm going to be leaving for good, Joey, me lad. No sense hanging around when things are the way they ought to be. When everything is settled up and there are no loose ends, a man can rest. If his conscience is clear, of course."

"Does that really make a difference?" asked Pete.

"Does it! I could tell you stories about friends of mine who will *never* get straightened out, because of the things they can't forget, things that weigh on their minds and will for all eternity."

"You wouldn't want to tell us, would you, George? We got nothing much to do today, have we, Pete?"

"Not a thing, Joe, and this is our last chance, George. If we do ten shovels apiece deeper, instead of six, would you tell us?"

"You boys get them bones buried right as rain and I'll have some time for you. We could go up by the old light and watch the river, so's I can always have the look of it in my mind. Don't know as I could spend a better day."

The boys did twenty shovels apiece till they were shoulder deep. Then they put some pine boughs in the bottom of the grave and laid the bones out, more or less the way they ought to have lain, only snugger. There were a lot of odds and ends they couldn't recognize, but they put the head at the top, and the arms along the sides, the ribs in the middle, then the legs. The odds and ends they laid neatly in the center. George's voice kept saying how pleased he was, and how grateful. Then they put some more pine boughs over the lot of them and began the filling in.

"Do you need any words said, George?" asked Joe.

"Well, now, boy, that's real nice of you to remember. I reckon it would make it more official and there sure weren't any words said last time, only a few cuss words. You might each think a little prayer or something."

"Does it matter what kind, George? I'm Catholic and Pete here is some kind of Protestant—"

"Presbyterian," corrected Pete.

"You fellers each say one of your own kind and that'll do fine. I didn't get around to go to much of any church in the old days, so the brand won't matter. You might say 'em silent-like. That'll do first rate."

So the boys said a prayer apiece and when they raised their heads they looked over to the place where the voice had been coming from. Only now George was standing there again and his face was one great smile. "That sure was mighty right and nice."

After that it didn't take them very long to finish the job. They were agreed that it would be better not to put any stones or marker over the spot, since, in the summertime, the Staats family came back once in a while to the burying ground and they might wonder about a new grave. Instead they pulled some vines over the place and piled up some leaves that were blown into a corner. Then they stood back a way and found that they had done a good job of concealment.

"Let's go ask my mother for some sandwiches and tell her we're going up to the other end of the island to explore. Will you come, George?"

"Today I'll do whatever you lads want me to."

"We want to hear about your friends, the ones who can't rest on account of their consciences," Pete said.

Not Quite Martin

By LEON WILSON

On the longest day of summer, or, to be absolutely exact, the shortest night of summer, Cody had a highly unusual adventure. Before I describe it, you need to know what Cody's favorite thing to eat was. Otherwise, you would never understand just how this exceedingly odd adventure came about.

Have you ever looked at your tongue in the mirror after you've been eating huckleberries? Or maybe you've seen someone else's tongue. The berries color it blue for a while.

Well, when it's summer on Cumberland Mountain and every huckle bush is so full of berries you would make yourself dizzy if you tried to add up the berries on even a small bush—you should see this boy Cody's tongue. Talk about blue!

Sometimes when Cody says something to his mother after he's been eating huckleberries, Callie will say to him, "So help me, Cody, when you open your mouth I have to look twice to make sure I'm not looking at the sky."

This story is from This Boy Cody *by Leon Wilson*

And Milt will say: "I declare, our boy's half a fool for those things. He's the huckleberry-eatingest boy in Tennessee, I do believe."

And then Omalia will say (for of course Omalia always has an opinion about everything) : "My brother *is* a huckleberry!"

And Cody, when he hears this, will grin till the grin almost goes out of sight around his head. To Cody's way of thinking, remarks like these are the finest kind of compliments.

When winter hits the Mountain and the trees are glazed with ice and the ground is blanketed with snow, you might imagine Cody would be downhearted because there are no berries to be had. If so, you would be wrong. All winter he grins because he knows that spring is on its way and presently the trees will put out their bright new leaves, and the woods will once again be absolutely popping with luscious, juicy huckleberries.

Omalia will eat huckles any time she happens to walk past a bush of them, but she's nowhere near being the nut about them her brother is. *Her* favorite food, of course, is yellowed cornbread fresh from her mother's oven. Sometimes she will polish off a whole pan of it and squawk for more. She would eat the stuff by the hour if her mother would ever bake that much of it for her.

Cody makes an effort to understand how his sister can be so daffy on the subject of cornbread, but for the life of him he can't. "Cornbread!" he says scornfully. "I believe I'd rather go hungry than have that crumbly stuff in my mouth!"

Pretty big talk, this, but don't get the idea that it bothers Omalia any, for it never does. You see, Omalia feels the same way about Cody's berry enthusiasm. When she sees her brother pass up a steaming chunk of cornbread running with butter because he's saving space for berries, she's apt to say something like:

"Poor Cody, he's huckle-touched."

Think this worries Cody? Not a bit! According to Cody, Omalia is cornbread-cracked. If she wasn't, he thinks, she would understand why he can never stop when he starts throwing down huckleberries.

And Cody believes his father can't understand because his father's favorite food in all the world is "leather breeches."

Bet a nickel you never heard of leather breeches till this minute. They're a very special kind of string beans. On hot summer days, Callie will spread ordinary string beans in the sun and leave them there till they shrivel and shrink to almost nothing and become as tough as pieces of leather. Then when winter comes, she'll put a pinch of these tough little almost-nothings in a pot, boil the daylights out of them, and they'll turn into string beans again, but the toughest, leatheriest string beans you ever flipped a lip over.

The reason Milt has such a fondness for these beans

is that they last a while. He likes something he can chew—something that won't disappear the minute you put it in your mouth. And say, for chewing, leather breeches beat anything you can think of. Take my word for it, they need *chewing* before they ever disappear!

Sometimes when Milt is enjoying a mess of good old tough leather breeches, he will get to thinking about Cody's powerful taste for huckleberries, and he will say:

"Cody, for the life of me, I don't see how you can eat so *many* of those things. I can understand eating a hand ful or two, or even a pailful, but not the slathers *you* put away. The way I look at it, when you eat one huckleberry, you've eaten them all. Don't they all taste the same?"

When Milt goes on like this, Cody buttons his lips and says nothing, for he feels exactly the same about his father's leather breeches. He thinks an ordinary person couldn't taste the difference between one leather breech and another if he tried all day, and he believes his father is just a little bit leather-breeches-loony or he would admit that this is the case.

What's more, Cody does not agree that all huckles taste alike. There are good ones, he feels, and better ones—better-than-ever ones, and best-yet ones. Anybody, he thinks, ought to be able to taste the different qualities—well, anybody who isn't crazy-wild about cornbread or else completely hipped on breeches!

47

Well, you now know the favorite eats of all the Cap-shaws but Callie. Truth to tell, she has no *absolutely* favorite food. She likes lots of things: ice-cold butter-milk, asparagus, potato soup, persimmons, rhubarb pie, peanut butter—I could go on all day, for Callie isn't one-sided like the rest of her family. You might say she will eat whatever comes along.

Well now, about this adventure Cody had.

You couldn't guess what it was if you guessed all week:

He didn't consume a lot of huckleberries that weren't ripe and come down with the bellyache.

And Milt didn't tell him to quit eating so many but he ate them anyway.

And he didn't fall over a cliff reaching for some that were growing far out at the tip of a branch.

No, this was a *real* adventure. Before I tell you about it, you've got to understand how Cody goes berrying. Then you will know how one thing led to another.

Suppose you lived on Cumberland Mountain and you were about ninety-eight per cent goofy on the sub-ject of huckleberries. Probably you would set out any old way and ramble from bush to bush till you had eaten all you could hold.

Not Cody, though! He was afraid he might miss a bush, so he had a scientific system. It was to keep go-ing to the right in a spiral that kept getting bigger. This way, he picked every bush in every direction. If he ever missed one, I doubt if the sun knew where it was to shine on it, or the bees could find it to draw the honey from its flowers.

And of course each year as Cody grew bigger, he could hold more huckleberries. Each year he spiraled farther and farther through the woods hunting them.

This particular day that Cody had his adventure, Omalia kept begging him to let her come along. She wasn't much interested in berries, though she would have eaten eight or ten dozen—she just wanted to be with Cody.

"You play with your dolls," Cody said. "I've got some mighty important business to take care of."

"Pretty-please," Omalia said. "I won't be a burr in your wool."

"No, Sister," Cody said. "I've got this afternoon all planned and you're not in it."

He didn't like having to be sharp with Omalia, but he knew she would keep begging him if he wasn't. She might even follow him after he stopped watching her.

"We'll do something tomorrow," he told her. "I won't be so huckleberry-hungry then. We'll finish building that house for Midnight, or we'll find us another bee tree."

"Promise?"—Omalia wanted to be sure.

"If the sun comes up tomorrow, it's a promise," Cody said. "If there's a stronger promise, I don't know it to give it to you."

So Cody got away from Omalia. He had to be even

crosser to get rid of Daybreak, for Daybreak had his mind strongly made up to go along.

Cody knew that if he gave in, Daybreak would undoubtedly discover a skunk and pester it till the worst happened. Or if he didn't find a skunk, he would step smack on the only mud-dauber for miles around and get his foot stung. Anyway, he would do some dumb thing that would be no help to scientific huckleberrying.

So Cody shied a stick at Daybreak and made him yelp.

"Home, you homely varmint!" he shouted, and Daybreak changed his mind in a hurry about accompanying Cody.

And this is how this boy Cody came to set out the way he wanted to be—alone.

Round and round he went in his big spiral till he got so far away from home that when night fell, he couldn't get home again.

And this is how his adventure began.

Of course the minute Cody took time off from his huckleberries to notice how dark it was getting, he began streaking for home as fast as he could go.

But as he put everything he had into burning up the miles, he knew he was being foolish. By this, I mean he knew for certain he couldn't make it home by suppertime. He had purposely saved up the longest day of summer for this huckleberry spree, remember, so he was now farther away from home than he had ever been before. And darkness was coming on fast, the way it always seems to when you don't want it to.

It wasn't long before Cody, instead of running between trees, was running into them.

"Ouch!" he cried when he hit the first one, then— "OUCH!"

After colliding with five trees, Cody quit running and began thinking. "I'm sure not getting home," he said to himself, "and I *am* getting a beaut of a bump on my noggin. What shall I do?"

Don't make a mistake now and think Cody was lost, for he wasn't. He knew perfectly well which way home was. All he needed to get there was a light. But he needed a lot more light than the fifteen matches he had in his pocket. They wouldn't have lasted him five minutes.

Had this been a night for the moon to come up, he could have proceeded easily, but there wasn't a sliver of a moon. This particular night was so absolutely totally black Cody couldn't even see the end of his nose. (He tried it—he looked cross-eyed to see if he could see it, but all he could see was night!)

Now if you were alone in the woods and it was pitch black dark, maybe you would be a little frightened. Cody wasn't, though. He knew all about the woods and being alone in the dark didn't worry him a bit. Of course he would have *preferred* being home with Milt and Callie and Omalia, but since this was out, he didn't intend to waste time wishing he was some place he couldn't be.

What he had to do was decide how and where to spend the night.

He wasn't sleepy yet because it wasn't bedtime, and he wasn't cold because it was midsummer, and he wasn't hungry because he was cram-jam full of his favorite food. All these things he wasn't. The main thing he *was* was tired of bumping into trees.

Now just as the last speck of daylight had vanished, Cody had sighted a little log cabin in which no one lived.

This is how he knew no one lived in it—

First thing: no light in the window.

Second thing: no smoke looping out of the chimney.

Third thing: no one moving around inside the cabin. Cody found *this* out by putting his ear to a crack in the logs and listening.

He couldn't hear a sound.

"Here's me my home for tonight," says Cody to himself, mighty proud of his cleverness, and he climbs the steps to the door, and just to make *completely* sure no one is inside, he knocks loudly.

No answer.

(He would have been mighty surprised, of course, if there had been an answer!)

So he pushes the door open and takes a look inside. But you can bet he doesn't see much, for it's as dark in there as the inside of a cow.

He lights one of his matches and looks again. And sees?—nothing. Or almost nothing. Just an old empty cabin. Not a chair or a table in it, not a lamp, a dish, or a bed. A few old sticks lying around on the floor to make a fire with, and that's all.

So in pops Cody, mighty pleased with himself, and shuts the door and scrammishes together some wood and makes himself a fire in the fireplace.

"Why shucks," he says to himself, "this is almost as good as being home. The only thing I lack here that I would have at home (besides a dish of the huckleberry pie my mother was baking) is someone to talk to. Too bad I hit ol' Daybreak with that stick. I should have let him come along—I'd have me some company now."

And now, listen:

The very minute he thinks about company, there comes a *tap-tap-tap* on the cabin door.

Very soft. So soft Cody hardly hears it. *So* soft Cody believes he has gone to sleep and he's dreaming that he heard it.

And now it comes again. A little louder this time. About like this: TAP-TAP-TAP.

This time Cody knows he's really hearing something. "Who in the world can be out there?" he asks himself. "Can't be anyone coming to see *me,* for who knows I'm here? Nobody!" He scratches his head to help himself think. "Maybe," he decides, "it's someone come to visit whoever it is that doesn't live here any more."

53

And now on the door there comes a good loud TAP-TAP-TAPPETY-TAP.

(Whoever's out there, he's getting tired of waiting. He's wanting an answer.)

"Open the door and come in, sir," Cody says politely. "Whoever you are, come in and enjoy my good fire with me."

Cody hears the door begin to open. He turns his head and peeks over his shoulder. And sees—

Not a man—

Not a woman—

Not a boy—

And no, not even a girl—

He sees a cat. A gray stripy cat with a long stripy tail.

The instant Cody sees it he knows it is no ordinary cat. For one thing, its yellow eyes are bigger and brighter and yellower by a good deal than an ordinary cat's are. For another thing, this cat's whiskers are longer and its gray stripy tail is *much* longer than even Midnight's, and Midnight's is pretty long.

I haven't told you yet how surprised Cody is, but you can imagine!

He's so surprised, in fact, seeing a cat walk in when he expected to see a man, that he now says to the cat the very thing he had planned to say to the man.

"Good evening, sir," he says.

And the little cat switches his long stripy tail and

looks Cody over with his big bright yellow eyes and replies as polite as you please:

"Good evening to *you, sir.*"

Cody is really surprised this time! He has seen clever cats before. Midnight, for instance. If no one is around to help Midnight, she will push a door open when she wants in or pull it open when she wants out. But clever as Midnight is, she doesn't talk! Cody guesses mighty few cats are clever enough to talk, and he decides to keep an eye on this one and see what clever thing it will do next.

But the cat doesn't do much more. It pushes the door shut, but then that's no great feat for even an ordinary cat. Then it strolls to the hearthstone and plumps down where it's warm from the fire and tucks its paws under its chest, the way a cat will. And it curls its long stripy tail around itself, and that's all.

Or just about all. One thing more: it turns its big bright eyes on Cody and gives him one of those long-lasting looks cats are so good at.

Cody grins at the little critter, hoping it will feel at home and talk some more, but the cat says not another word. It yawns one of those gaping yawns cats go in for and then it returns to watching Cody's fire. And this time, this is really all it does.

"Pretty nice fire, isn't it?" Cody remarks. He's out to make the little thing talk.

Does the cat reply? It does not! Does the cat even

look at Cody again? It does not! It goes on watching the fire for all the world as if it hadn't heard Cody speak.

Cody shakes his head. "What a crying shame!" he says to himself. He's pretty sure he's never going to meet another cat clever enough to talk. Too bad this one won't open up so he can find out what cats think about.

And now on the cabin door comes a *rap-rap-rap*. Not loud, but louder than the cat's tap-tap-tap. About like this: RAP-RAP-RAP.

"Well!" says Cody to himself. "Who is it this time? Someone looking for the man who doesn't live here any more, or another cat?"

Cody thinks it would be dandy if another talking cat came in. Might be just what this fellow on the hearthstone needs to get him going. Then while the two cats discussed cat matters together, he could sit here and listen and learn.

RAPPETY-RAP-RAP-RAP! Good and loud this time—and Cody realizes that with all his wondering who it is, he's been keeping the rapper waiting. He pops his mouth open to say "Come in, whoever you are," but before he has a chance to say it, the cat on the hearthstone cries out:

"You're wasting your time rapping—open and enter!"

Before Cody can get over his surprise at this, he has to peek over his shoulder again, for the door is opening.

A man this time?

No.

Another cat, then?

No, not another cat.

A big old smiling possum!

Chances are you've never seen a possum. If you haven't, you've missed something. Possums' eyes are small, almost as small as apple seeds, and their mouths are famous for the very long thin white teeth in them, and possums are famous too for their tails which are not only long and thin but almost completely hairless.

And here's another thing: most any time you see a possum, it will seem to be smiling, only his smile isn't the kind you and I give out when we're happy about something. It's a special, quite unhappy sort of smile and yet not altogether unhappy—about half and half, as if the possum had a bellyache but didn't mind it. Rather liked it, in fact. Possums seem to be saying with this special sickly smile of theirs: "Oh, I feel *so* sick, and I do hope *you* feel the same."

Cody has seen possums before this, of course, for there are lots of them on Cumberland Mountain, but in all his life he has never seen such a possumy-looking possum as this one coming in the door. Never has he seen such *very* long sharp teeth or such a completely sickly smile.

And what does this most possumy-looking possum do? It shuts the door and then comes creeping across the floor in that slow-going, take-it-easy way possums

have, and slides in beside the cat. Then it looks up at
Cody with its eyes that are like two shiny apple seeds,
and of course it continues to smile its half-happy, half-
unhappy bellyache smile. And now it turns to the cat
and asks in a take-it-easy possum sort of drawl:

"How soon?" and at the same time it jerks its head
toward Cody so the cat will know what it's talking
about.

The cat glances up at Cody with his bright golden
eyes and says to the possum, as plain as you please:

"We can't do nothin' till Martin comes."

Then it yawns another one of those tremendous cat
yawns and goes back to watching Cody's fire.

This seems to satisfy the possum. Smiling its bellyache smile, it says not another word and commences
watching the fire.

Cody politely waits for the cat and the possum to
say something more, even though he has a question
troubling him. "Excuse me, please," he says finally.

The cat and the possum look up to find out what's on
Cody's mind.

"I heard you mention Martin," Cody says. "Who *is*
Martin, and about how soon do you reckon he'll be
coming along?"

The cat looks at the possum but says nothing. The
possum looks at the cat and says nothing. They both
look at Cody—silently. Then they look back at the fire.

So all Cody can do is wonder about Martin.

And as he wonders, he finds himself beginning to

feel mighty regretful about something—what he said to Omalia. "The next time that girl asks to go somewhere with me," he says to himself, "by golly, I'm going to let her. Right now, company is something I'd like to have, and I don't mean this four-legged company."

And now, on the door:

Scrape-scrape-scrape.

This time Cody finds he isn't much interested in saying "Come in, whoever you are." Maybe it's Martin, and maybe he doesn't care to see Martin coming in, making himself at home. The more Cody thinks it may be Martin, the more he wants to think no one is outside at all, so he tries his level best to believe that the wind is blowing a tree branch against the door. Of course the scraping noise is a bit loud for a branch, especially when there isn't a breath of wind stirring—but Cody thinks there's no harm in trying.

Now here it comes again, much louder:

SCRAPE-SCRAPE-SCRAPE.

(It certainly isn't a tree branch!)

"Kick it open and join us!" the possum calls out in a loud voice, and the little cat cries out:

"We're waiting for you!"

This time, as the door opens, Cody takes his time peeking around. He isn't by any means certain he wants to see who is coming in.

And who is? Another cat? Another possum? Martin, maybe?

Not quite.

When Cody gets his eyes around, he sees a sleek red fox with high pointed ears, a long pointed nose, shiny at the tip, and eyes as glittery as two polished black marbles. And a tail so bushy and long that it's almost the size of the fox.

And what does he do, this fox who is bigger than the possum who in turn is bigger than the little cat? Well, he doesn't do anything, unless you want to call shutting the door something.

He steps quieter than a whisper across to the hearthstone and glides in beside the possum. Then he swings his rusty red head Cody's way and slowly winks one of his glittery black eyes for all the world as if he and Cody are sharing some deep secret.

Then he turns to the possum and the cat and in his super-sleek soft foxy voice, he asks:

"How soon?"

And the cat and the possum answer, "We can't do nothin' till Martin comes."

"Oh," says the fox, and once again he looks up at Cody and slyly winks one eye.

And while the fox winks, the possum smiles his belly-ache smile, and the little cat stares at Cody with his bright yellow eyes that every minute seem to grow a little bigger.

And all the time the animals are watching Cody, Cody is thinking. He's thinking so hard about something good to eat that he can almost taste it.

Strangely enough, it isn't huckleberries. It's an enormous plate of yellow cornbread fixed up with butter and bee honey. And right beside the steaming hot cornbread is a dish piled high with—have you guessed? —leather breeches. And just beyond the breeches sits a glass of ice-cold buttermilk at least ten inches tall.

What a slam-gorgeous supper, Cody thinks—my, if only I was home this minute with my ears pinned back, eating such a supper, I wouldn't be here in this crowded old cabin that's getting more crowded every minute. Boy, what I wouldn't give for a mess of cornbread!

And right in the middle of Cody's cornbread thinking:

CRACKETY-BANG!

The door again, and this time it doesn't begin to sound like a branch scraping in the wind. All it sounds like is someone in a burning hurry to enter.

"Kick it open and roll in!" cries the fox.

"Waitin' for you!" cries the possum.

"Me too!" cries the cat.

When Cody peeks over his shoulder this time, he sees a panther!

(Now if you've never seen a panther, an easy way to imagine what this one looked like is to think how that little cat beyond the possum would look if it wasn't little but gigantic.)

What a whopper of a panther this one coming in the door is! His ears are as big as Easter baskets. His eyes are as bright as two flashlights. His whiskers stick out

61

like knitting needles. His tail is so long Cody wonders
if it's ever going to end. (It does end, but not for a
long time.)

And what does the panther do? Nothing much. He
shuts the door of course—but then they all shut the
door—and he stalks to the hearthstone and moves in
beside the fox.

Then he turns his flashlight eyes on Cody and he
looks the boy up, looks him down, looks him back, looks
him forth, and after he's looked at Cody all these ways,
he turns to the fox and the possum and the cat and, in
a gigantic, panthery voice, he says just one word:

"When?"

And the cat and the possum and the fox all reply
at once:

"We can't do nothin' till Martin comes!"

Now all the time this is going on, something else
has been happening that I haven't had a chance to mention: Cody's fine fire has been burning lower and lower
the way any fire will when you fail to feed it. By now,
the fire is so low and the cabin is so dark that when
Cody looks at his four visitors, this is just about all
he can see:

The stary yellow eyes of the little cat—

The shiny apple-seed eyes of the smiling possum—

The glittery marble eyes of the fox (one of them
slowly winking from time to time)—

And the flashlight eyes of the panther—

And all those eyes are looking straight at Cody!

So Cody scrammishes around in a hurry and builds up his fire. He wants to see more than just eyes. Yes sir, as long as he has to sit here, he wants a good view of the folks he's sitting with.

And now at the door there is a new noise—not a tap, not a *rap,* not a SCRAPE, not a CRACKETY-BANG but one tremendous—

CRASH!

as the door flies back and in springs the biggest old black bear Cody has ever seen. He's two sizes bigger than the biggest bear Cody has ever even *dreamed* of seeing, and he's three shades blacker, and his black shiny eyes look as big as doorknobs.

And what does he do, this bear of all bears? One thing he doesn't do: he doesn't shut the door. Hasn't time. Too big a hurry.

One spring and he's on the hearthstone beside the panther, and he's looking Cody over with his doorknob eyes, but not for long, because he has to find out something in a hurry—right now! He turns to quiz the panther, the fox, the possum, and the cat, but before he can say anything, they all reply at once:

"We can't do nothin' till Martin comes!"

"Thanks for telling me," says the bear in a booming, bear sort of voice, and he turns to look at Cody again.

But now, what's this? Where is Cody?

The animals look around the cabin quickly, thinking maybe he has run away.

But Cody hasn't gone anywhere—not yet. He's standing in the middle of the cabin looking down at his feet, and anyone can see that something about his feet is worrying him.

As the animals watch, Cody begins stamping. One foot and then the other. He makes quite a bit of noise with them.

The animals look at one another in amazement. "What's the big idea?" they seem to be saying. "Why this stamping? Why isn't this boy Cody sitting here enjoying this good fire with us while we wait for Martin?"

And perhaps you are wondering.

I'll tell you:

Back when the panther came stalking in, Cody began to feel an itchy sensation in his feet that wouldn't go away. In fact, the longer he sat on the hearthstone doing nothing to get rid of the sensation, the itchier it became. By the time the bear burst in, Cody's feet were itching him so bad he couldn't sit still another second.

That's why he's stamping now in the middle of the cabin.

"Itch in my feet," he informs the bewildered animals. He can tell from the way they look at him that they don't believe a word of it. The yellow eyes of the little cat and the possum's apple seeds and the fox's glittery marbles and the panther's flashlights and the bear's doorknobs are all as full of disbelief as they can be.

"Young Mr. Cody seems not to care for our company," the animals appear to be saying.

Cody is sorry they don't believe him, but he doesn't see what he can do about it. After all, he's telling them the truth—it's their tough luck if they won't believe him.

"Stamping helps some," he goes on, "but not enough. I believe I've got to walk some. Walk fast. This little cabin isn't half big enough for the walking I've got to do. I'd be hitting the walls six times a minute, trying to do my walking in here."

All the time Cody is explaining this, he's backing slowing to the door, and now he stands with one of his itchy feet outside on the steps, waiting to go.

"Friends," he says—and his feet are so impatient he can hardly stand still long enough to say this one more thing he wants to say—"friends," he says quietly and politely, "when Martin gets here, tell him I was here, please, and tell him I waited as long as I could, but I couldn't wait one minute more."

And saying this, Cody commences his fast walk away from the cabin, and do you know?—the minute he looks back and sees that the cat and the possum and the fox and the bear aren't following him, his feet practically entirely stop itching!

Well, that's the adventure Cody had the day he ate more huckleberries than he had ever eaten before.

The sun was coming up as he started his swift departure from that cabin, so it wasn't a great time before he was home again, eating breakfast with Milt and Callie and Omalia. Between bites of pie (for Cody's breakfast was a piece of the huckle pie he had missed out on the night before), Cody told his story exactly as I have told it: how he met the cat, the possum, the fox, the panther, the bear, and almost but not quite Martin. The minute he finished, Omalia, who had been listening pop-eyed to every word, exclaimed:

"Fiddle faddle! You made it up to give us a thrill."

"Made it up!" Cody said indignantly.

"Possums don't talk," Omalia said, "and neither do cats or panthers or foxes or bears."

"*This* possum talked," Cody said, "and so did the rest of them. Shucks, they talked all kinds of stuff."

Omalia shook her head and looked exceedingly wise for a little girl of seven. "I suspect," she said sternly, "you went in that cabin and fell asleep and dreamed every bit of it."

"Dreamed it?" Cody cried. "You wouldn't have thought it was a dream if you'd been there!"

Omalia went right on as if she hadn't heard Cody. "In fact," she said, addressing her mother and father, "I've made up my mind it was a dream. Cody must have eaten some green huckleberries and they didn't sit right."

"Dream!" Cody muttered, spooning up the pie juice on his plate. "Green huckleberries!" Suddenly his face puckered up with thought.

"What's the matter, Cody?" his mother asked. She feared Cody might not be feeling well, having been up so late the night before.

"Nothing's the matter," Cody said. "I'm thinking."

"Thinking what?" Milt asked, for he could see that Cody was pretty worried.

"He's thinking how glad he is we saved him this little ol' slab of pie," Omalia suggested.

"I'm thinking," Cody said slowly, "maybe my feet shouldn't have gotten itchy just when they did. Golly, the very *next* one might have been Martin himself. Now I'll always wonder who Martin was and never know."

"Dreams like that," Omalia said in her most grown-up tone, "always disappoint you when you wake up."

No sooner had she said this than there came a strange thumping noise at the front door. Omalia's heart almost jumped out of her mouth! Quickly she reached for the cream pitcher so Cody wouldn't see how startled she was.

But Cody was watching the door, not his sister. The door was opening, slowly, mysteriously. Cody felt the hair on the back of his neck begin to creep. He held his breath.

And Omalia forgot completely about the cream and held her breath!

And the door swung wide and in walked—

Yes, a cat—but this time the cat was a normal-looking, non-talking cat with regulation-size eyes. Just Midnight looking for breakfast.

Cody sighed in relief. Then he looked at his mother and father and Omalia. "Dream or not," he said, grinning, "that's exactly the way it started!"

Dead Men on Parade

By IRVING CRUMP

It was Master Diver Arthur Davis who told me the story of the dead men on parade. Davis has roamed the seven seas as an expert diver for a Pacific Coast wrecking company and has had many strange experiences under water. But the most thrilling of all occurred when he went down to the wreck of the tramp steamer *El Songo* in one of the Atlantic sea lanes, to secure the bodies of five of the fire-room crew who had been trapped in the vessel when she foundered.

"I was working for a salvage and wrecking company that handled all kinds of jobs and I, with my buddies, who tend pump and take care of my lines, were dispatched to the scene of the accident as quickly as possible," he told me.

"Those buddies of mine were divers too; old fellows at the game who had passed their diving days. One of them had been a good man until he had let drink rob him of most of the vitality that he needed in the hard underwater work. The others were men past thirty-five

This story is from Boys' Life *magazine*

who had worn themselves out in the work; for a man spends a lot of physical and nervous energy, and is often 'old' in his middle thirties at the work of diving.

"They take to tending lines and pumps then and serving younger fellows who go down. They know exactly what they must do for the best interest of the diver under the surface. The man at the lines can tell from the pressure on them and the signals sent up to him just how the man 'under' is faring, while those at the pumps know to a nice point just how much or how little air must be supplied at various depths for the perfect comfort of the diver.

"We reached the scene of the wreck at mid-day, and although there was a strong swell running, it was not rough enough to interfere with work, and I proceeded with the assistance of my helpers to hurry into my rig because the tide was just at the beginning of the low water slack.

"You know what a diving outfit looks like. It's a big rubber suit; like a pair of hip boots attached to a seamless jacket of rubber with big sleeves. It fits snug about the neck and wrist, particularly at the wrists where it grips the flesh tight half-way up the forearm so that the water cannot enter the suit in that way. At the neck it is reinforced by a big rubber ring or collar that is slipped over your head and made fast. This is really a rubber gasket that fits snugly against a copper collar to which the helmet is bolted. The helmet is of copper with three windows or eyes; lenses of glass reinforced with mesh wire so that they cannot be easily broken. Two on either side are permanently fixed in the helmet. The third or front window screws into place.

"From the copper helmet leads the air pipe and safety line which are carried down the back and up under each arm, coming up in front and being made fast to lugs on the helmet. Some helmets are also fitted with telephone equipment and the wire runs parallel with the air pipe and safety lines under the diver's arms. Many divers do not like the telephone sets because they are of little use, except in special work, and their trailing wire is only another line to become entangled. I never use one when I can help it. In addition to this equipment there are, of course, the weighted shoes, each no lighter than thirty pounds, and the weighted belt of a hundred pounds or more.

"It was that identical rig I crawled into; took my battery lamp, because I was going down better than seventy feet where the light is not the best, and climbing over the side, waited a moment while my helmet was being adjusted, the face plate screwed into place, and my buddy tapped on the top of my copper dome telling me that all was ready for the descent.

"I started down the ladder, the cold water lapping at my knees, then my hips, then up under my arms and gurgled past my copper dome. I was under. Three rungs down the ladder I climbed, then stepped off into space and let go. Down I dropped. Down, down, down into the greenish amber depths. I didn't fall like a plummet. Rather I floated pleasantly downward leaving a string of glowing silver bubbles in my wake from the exhaust air escaping from the safety valve in the copper dome and trickling out around my wrists.

"It was no new sensation to me. I had done it a hundred times before. I always like the descent. I have such a pleasant feeling of floating comfortably downward. Fifty feet I dropped. The depths began to get more shadowy; more weird and ghostly. Long tentacles of green and amber kelp floated upward, waving gracefully in the water. Startled fish darted here and there in confusion, looking with goggled-eyed wonder at the strange monster descending into their world. They were big fish, too; cods, three feet long, and longer; haddock, their scales glowing purple and bronze and white in the weird light as they flashed past me. There were sharks too; but not the man-eating kind. They were the dog-fish variety, cowardly fish that darted away with the rest of the scaly denizens.

"Half-way down the pressure made my ears snap and with the snapping whatever unpleasant sensations I felt on the descent disappeared entirely. It is always that way. With the increased pressure of the water a diver feels a strain on his ears until they reach a point where there is a sharp crack in each of them. With that they automatically adjust themselves to the new pressure and there is no further feeling of discomfort. The man whose ears do not act that way is never a successful diver. If he persists in the work, sooner or later he will have a hemorrhage.

"Then I settled comfortably on the bottom; a firm white sandy bottom, across which huge crabs and giant lobsters scuttled with their awkward, spiderish strides. Some of those lobsters were so large and their nippers were so big and ugly looking, that I gave them plenty of room. It would be an easy matter for one of them to shear through my rubber suit with a single nip, and then a hole in a diving suit is a mighty serious thing.

"I had landed in a sandy opening in what was a veritable submarine forest. Giant fronds of kelp and other varieties of seaweed waved gracefully overhead; high overhead, some of them reaching upward forty or fifty feet toward that great amber greenish window above me. It is pretty down there darting in and out among the shadows and somehow the string of silvery bubbles always trailing upward from my helmet seems to add to the picture.

"But I had little time to admire the scenery. A great skate flapped slowly across the sandy opening looking curiously at me, but as I stepped toward him he darted off into the forest. From soundings made I knew the ill-fated tramper lay somewhere to my left and I started in that direction. But I had scarcely entered the jungle of seaweed when I came upon her with her great nose hanging over the edge of a submarine cliff or shelf that fell away—I could not guess to what depth.

"I began to explore the steel sides to see if there was any external evidence of what had happened to the vessel. The bubbles from my air lodged against the seams between the steel plates of the vessel and along each line of rivets and glowed phosphorescently, outlining big sections of the vessel. I worked my way down the sta'board side as far as I could without stepping off the subterranean cliff. Twice some action of the water made the vessel roll heavily, then settle back into its grave. It reminded me of a huge animal trying to summon its death-relaxed muscles to action.

"Five minutes of exploring and I found what had happened. There had evidently been an explosion inside the vessel on the sta'board side. Steel plates were bent and buckled and lines of rivets had been torn away. The vessel had filled with water and gone down immediately. Only a few of the deck crew and the officers had been able to save themselves.

"I retraced my steps then and working around the stern started down the port side to find a handy place to climb up on deck. The boat had such a heavy list to port that I had little difficulty scrambling up and finding the fire-room hatchway. Indeed I had scarcely gone a dozen feet along the deck when I glimpsed the hatchway. The top had been blown back by the explosion and through the opening appeared a single human hand and naked forearm. Accustomed as I am to gruesome underwater sights, that white hand with its pathetically groping, futilely clutching fingers moving eerily back and forth across the edge of the hatch with the action of the water, as if waving me a signal, made me shudder.

"I scrambled over the sloping deck and presently I was kneeling beside the hatch and peering into that black chamber of horrors below.

"The body of a seaman, naked to the waist, blocked the entrance. He was twisted in such a position that I could not pull him through, and in order to get in I had to shove him back with my foot.

"I climbed down the ladder then, and reached the listing fire-room floor. Then I flashed on my electric lamp.

"They were all there, the whole fire-room crew; five of them, and gathered almost at the foot of the ladder, like a spectral reception committee waiting to receive me. Poor fellows, they stared at me with eyes wide open and horror-stricken as they had faced death. Their expressions for the most part were terrible to behold, though I saw one or two who had died with a grim smile on his lips. One had played the coward. He had a Navy automatic in his hand and there was an ugly blue hole in his temple. There was one caught between two lockers in a kneeling position. How he got there I do not know, but I always like to believe that he met death just that way, uttering a last prayer to his Maker. There was no look of terror on his white face, and his eyes, of them all, were peacefully closed.

"To get these bodies out and up to the surface was my first consideration. But I put off beginning the task until I had explored the boiler-room. They had said that there were five men trapped in there, but there might be more. The whole crew of the tramper was far from accounted for.

"I moved slowly forward. But the swirling suction I made in the water started all the five dead men moving. They fell in behind me; close behind me, like dead men on parade, with me as their accepted leader. Some of them bumped against me. Even the kneeling man between the lockers rolled toward me and seemed to reach outward to grasp my legs. Two floated upward and seemed to hover over my head, dangling their hands in my face.

"Working under a high nervous tension, as all divers do, this exasperated me. I knew exactly why the dead men moved, and an emotion akin to anger welled up within me. There was nothing for me to do but tie them all fast to something while I went about searching for their companions, otherwise they would follow me clear to the bow, if I went that far. I found some rope and tied them all fast, every last one of them. Then I proceeded with my investigations.

"As I worked my way forward I began to see huge repulsive-looking conger eels, gliding through the blackness within the hull. I knew what they were after. It made me angry. I ground one of the slimy things under my iron-shod heels.

"I was well down the fire-room. Just as I was in the act of turning back, convinced that all the fire-room victims of the disaster were gathered in a group at the ladder where they had rushed when the explosion sounded, the ship gave a rolling lurch again, then settled back as it had done twice while I was crawling around outside. But with the motion came a sudden silence that made me grow sick. The far-off thump of the pumps and the coughing of air coming into my helmet had ceased. My air line was fouled; perhaps cut! What had happened?

"Swiftly and with a little suggestion of panic, I turned back amidships, following my pipe line. It was whole up to the point where it led in through the hatchway. A moment later I knew what had happened.

"The lurch of the ship had thrown the hatch cover back into place again. The seaman's body and the list of the ship had prevented that from happening before, but now that the man's body had been removed, the lid had fallen down into place again and had pinched—perhaps cut my air-pipe line.

"Sick with horror, I climbed the fire-room ladder as fast as the water would let me, while the whole sepulchral crew of dead men seemed to turn and watch me with their horrible staring eyes. I got a small measure of hope in the fact that the pipe line had not been cut, at least. I was getting just a little air—a very, very little, however. I understood why in a moment. Fortunately for me, several strands of steel hoisting cables had been hanging down the hatchway and this had prevented the hatch cover from cutting my pipe line,

But the swirling suction started the dead men moving . . .

though it had pinched it severely and had clamped down on my safety line so hard that I could not send a distress signal to the pumps. Already I was breathing the stale, vitiated air that I had breathed before. I was gasping and panting. My famished lungs were hurting me, crying out in pain for more and fresher air. I must free that pipe from the pinch between the hatch cover and frame immediately, or my career as a diver would end in a matter of minutes.

"Bracing myself against the rungs of the ladder, I set all my strength against the hatch and shoved up-ward. But below the surface even the slightest task, such as driving a nail, requires tremendous physical exertion. Though I exerted all my strength, I could only budge the hatch a few inches. I could not open it entirely. My strength was unequal to it, for the tide had begun to flow, and that with the pressure of the water against the cover made the task of opening it something beyond mere physical strength.

"Until my heart was pounding like a trip-hammer and the blood was throbbing in my temples, I pushed against that hatch, and although I was able to release the pinch on my pipe line I could not throw it all the way open as it had been before.

"But at least I could save myself from immediate extinction. I managed somehow to jam the head of the hammer I always carried in my belt between the cover and the frame, and that held it open for a space of three inches, allowing ample room for my air pipe to clear.

"I was tired, terribly tired; and—yes, I'll admit it —frightened, too. I climbed down the ladder into the fire-room again and sat on a locker—the same one at which the seaman had been kneeling. I looked around at the ring of ghastly dead men who stood, hung and leaned drunkenly about me, as if watching me and wondering what I was going to do about the situation. I could almost imagine some of them grinning at me with ghastly, unpleasant grins. And as I watched them I could not help wondering whether I might not soon join that ghastly crew.

"But such thoughts were not good for me. I threw them off. I couldn't afford to sit there idly on the locker with death so close to me. There was little chance of my being rescued by my buddies above. There was no other complete diving equipment on the barge, and to wait until another diver and more equipment was sent for would take hours. I would be a lunatic by that time, I knew. I must do something to get out of that ship immediately. If I only had some sort of a serviceable tool. If I could find a jack, or a crowbar or something to help me, I might be able to pry that hatch off, or at least raise it enough so that I could crawl out.

"I began a systematic search of the fire-room. I broke open lockers and explored nook and corner. I was almost in despair when in a locker in the engine-room I found what I was looking for; a hand screw-jack. I shouted in ecstasy and my own voice boomed loud in the narrow confines of my copper helmet, as I took the powerful little instrument in my hands and started for the hatchway again. I'm not sure but that I exhibited my find to the staring dead men then. I think I even talked to them; told them that I wasn't going to join their sepulchral crew, after all, for you see, my nerves had been badly unstrung by the ordeal and I was suffering a reaction.

"What that screw-jack was used for on board the steamer I did not know. Nor did I care. I blessed the kind providence that had made it part of the vessel's equipment. It was a small one, scarcely five inches over all. But it was sufficient to serve my purposes. I built up a substantial bracing against the upper rung of the fire-room ladder, put the jack into place against the underside of the hatch cover, and with a short spike that fitted it as a handle I began to turn. It worked slowly; oh, so slowly. At first I could scarcely see the screw turn. But it was turning. My hammer fell from the angle into which it had been jammed and sank past me to the bottom of the ship. I watched the narrow slit of an opening, as it gradually widened. It was four inches, five inches, six inches. Presently I reached the limit of the jack. I left it braced as it was and returned to the engine-room of the steamer, where I found a steel bar that would hold the lid open, while I was readjusting the jack. Then I started the operation all over again.

"Wider the lid opened, and ever wider. Eight inches, ten inches, a foot of space yawned toward freedom.

Normally I could crawl through that much of an opening. But with my copper helmet on it was impossible. I must force the lid back still further.

"Once more I found a steel bar long enough to brace the lid open, and building up more bracings, set the screw-jack again. Inch by inch I raised that lid until it was braced open, quite wide enough to allow my big copper helmet to pass through the opening.

"I became so eager then that I began to tremble. I had to stand still once and pull myself together. Unless a man works with the utmost deliberation and coolness 'down under,' he is very likely to overlook some little thing that might in the end prove fatal to him.

"But I did not go down into the fire-room again to say farewell to those poor fellows who had not been as fortunate as I was. I would see them again, I felt certain. But for the present I had had quite enough of their company. I stood on the ladder and carefully passed out all my air-pipe and life line, and had it all coiled neatly on the listing deck. Then carefully I began to crawl out myself.

"But once I had cleared my copper helmet I knew that I could safely crawl through the opening, and in a few minutes I was standing on the sloping deck-plates, free of what might easily have been my death trap. I paused a moment there to sit down and compose myself. How good things looked out there in that soft greenish-amber light. How fortunate I was to be able to look at that great submarine forest again. I was ready to leave it now for a little time. But I would be back again; back with a bundle of gelatine sticks and a wire from a battery overhead, for I was determined that before I entered that fire-room once more I would blow the hatch cover off entirely with a high explosive. Then there would be no chance of my becoming trapped in there again."

The House of Ocean Born Mary

By MARION LOWNDES

All in a spirit of fun a Concord policeman and three other young men set out for Henniker, New Hampshire, on a certain night in October not many years ago.

When they got near Henniker, as far as the bridge over the Contoocook River, they turned right and, driving up an overgrown woods road, they parked the car where the woods broke on an open field. Then they waited—not that they really expected anything, but still, they had all heard strange tales of other October nights along this road.

The autumn frost was sucking the warmth from the ground in a wet vapor; out in the woods a fox barked and a bird croaked sleepily in a nearby birch. A yellow moon rose over the mountain behind them and outlined against the sky the high roofs of the Mary Wallace house where it stood dark and old in the misty field.

Then they saw it. A woman in white, a tall woman,

This story is from Ghosts *That Still Walk by Marion Lowndes*

Then they saw it—a woman in white . . .

was walking with a firm unhurried step toward the well under the old apple tree at the side of the house. She dropped something in, turned and came back in the direction of the road. That was all—but none of them saw where she went. She just wasn't there any more.

Years and years before this a man riding late into Henniker, also in October, had seen the same performance. At the time, the house was deserted. More recently, a farmer in the neighborhood had the same experience; also in October.

The Roys, who own the house now, have tried to investigate the well, without success. It seems to have no bottom, so whatever went in disappeared for good.

As for the woman in white, according to local information she is Mary Wallace, Ocean Born Mary Wallace, for whom the house was built in a lonely birch woods half way up the side of a mountain, south of Henniker.

She has been "seen" by at least seven people in the last hundred years and sensed by many more.

In her lifetime Ocean Born Mary was a famous character, as she has been ever since, in this part of New Hampshire. Her story starts more than two hundred years ago, when square riggers with the best of luck took six weeks to make an Atlantic crossing, and dreaded, if they spoke another sail, to see the terrible skull and crossbones suddenly run up on the masthead.

Even with fair weather and no pirates, the sea voyage

to America was an ordeal. There was no such thing as canned food or refrigeration; all perishable food had to be taken on salted or dried. Thirsty fare at best; and the water on these long voyages was horrible. They had none of our chemicals to keep it sterile, and worms and greens flourished in the kegs. People called it black water and sucked it through their clenched teeth. Below decks it was dark and dirty and when the winds rose the poor passengers were battened down and knocked about like ninepins, inside the high, pitching hulls of their clumsy square riggers.

In 1720 a schooner from Londonderry, Ireland, was proceeding slowly up the coast of Massachusetts, loaded with Irish colonists bound for Londonderry, New Hampshire, where their friends and relatives had settled before them. It had been a hard voyage, of course, but not an eventful one. A baby girl had been born at sea and both she and her mother were doing well enough in their dark, mildewy berth below. The other passengers were having a little pleasure at last, sitting or strolling about the high gunwaled decks, enjoying the sunshine and the soft off-shore breezes. They couldn't see the land, but it was near. Toward sunset on one of the last days a tall-masted ship bore down on them. She was narrow and sharp in the bow and painted black. The dreaded black flag flew from her masthead. Aboard the Irish schooner, Captain Wilson, the father of the ocean born baby, ordered his sails to be furled. Escape was impossible and they weren't armed to fight

87

it out. Perhaps if they surrendered right away they would have a chance of being let off. But the pirates, when they came aboard, were furious. The Irish colonists were poor people and carried no fine cargo of brandies and satins.

"Line your men up—passengers and crew—forward of the main mast," the pirate captain roared. His men called him Don Pedro, but he spoke perfect English. His hair and his mustachios and his eyebrows were very black and shaggy, and his sun-scorched skin showed dark and tight over his long breast bones where his linen shirt lay open. In his swarthy head the pale grey of his deep set eyes were startling; they never stayed fixed on any spot for long and they gave him a ferocious look, like a panther. Like a panther, too, he had a way of drawing back his lips in a nervous snarl that showed the teeth, very white against his moustaches.

"It's too bad you had nothing to make this little call worth-while," Don Pedro roared to the helpless company. "Since we haven't got anything out of you we're not going to take any risks. You're too near port for your own good. Every one of you is going to the bottom of the sea, *now*. Be ready to fire the ship," he added, to his own scowling, wildly dressed boat's crew.

The horror-struck silence that followed Don Pedro's speech was broken by a funny little howl floating up the companionway. All the tramping about had waked a hungry baby.

"What's that?" roared the pirate. "Go below and

bring it up," he ordered the man beside him. "And anything else you find."

In a few minutes Mrs. Wilson was on deck, with her tiny wailing baby wrapped in a blanket and pressed to her shoulder. She leaned weakly against the mast and fixed her eyes on the fierce, nervous figure of Don Pedro.

"Yours?" he asked.

Mrs. Wilson nodded.

"What do you call it?"

"She has no name."

"A girl, eh?" His lips twitched uneasily, and the thin sharp edges of his upper teeth flashed white. "Well, I might be a fool for once. If I should let you and this company go, will you name the baby Mary?"

"I promise I will," said Mrs. Wilson.

At her answer, Don Pedro looked almost pleased.

"Bring the boats alongside," he shouted, and the pirates swarmed overboard and rowed back to their black schooner.

Then, before they'd had time to unfurl their sails, the Irishmen saw Don Pedro returning. At first they supposed he had thought better of his offer, but the pirate captain only stood up in the stern sheets and hurled a bolt of cloth onto the schooner's deck.

"For Mary," he shouted, "for her wedding gown," and rowed away.

It was a piece of superb grey-green silk, strewn with tiny bright pink brocaded flowers, and Ocean Born

Mary, as she was always called, did wear it on her wedding day.

For years after their narrow escape none of the ship's company heard anything more of Don Pedro. Captain Wilson died while his daughter was still a child and her mother took her then to the lonely peace of Henniker, far from pirates and the sea.

When Ocean Born Mary grew up, stories of her beauty spread as far as Portsmouth. No one who saw her ever forgot her. She was very tall—almost six feet —her hair was an Irish red, her skin very white, and her dark-lashed eyes were as soft and as green as the moss in the Henniker woods. It was news all over New Hampshire when, at the age of twenty-two, she was married to Thomas Wallace. But one person was especially interested to hear of it, a lean, shifty-eyed old seaman who happened to be in Portsmouth at the time. He drew back his greying moustaches in his funny nervous way, and asked a stage driver to draw him a map so that he could see just where Henniker lay.

Ocean Born Mary lived quietly on her Henniker farm for a few happy years; then Thomas Wallace died, in his early middle age, leaving her young, beautiful and alone with five children. With no man to help them, the Wallace family were going to find the winters long and hard and the summers full of work. Ocean Born Mary's green eyes stared wide and frightened into the future.

She didn't know that in the first spring of her wid-ow-hood a barge had come slowly up the Contoocook River toward Henniker. It carried all sorts of tools and furnishings and four or five black slaves, a ship's car-penter, and a rough looking man who seemed to be a body servant for the owner of the barge—a lean, still handsome old man with pale glancing eyes set deep under his shaggy brows.

Even around Henniker, Don Pedro didn't like to at-tract too much attention. He hid his barge in a grove of alders and went on foot to call on Ocean Born Mary. They had a long talk and in the end she agreed to bring her family and come and stay with the old man in the house he was going to build, half way up the mountain, south of the town.

That house would have been the wonder of the neigh-borhood, except that people were leery of going there unless they had business. They did not trust those queer black slaves prowling round the house like so many wolves, or the profane, bad-tempered seaman with the knife in his belt; or, least of all, Don Pedro.

But Ocean Born Mary was happy enough in her lonely splendor. The house Don Pedro built was the perfect background for her. A big, generous, black house. The front door was canary yellow, battened with a Christian cross and a Crusader's cross, the like of which had never been seen around Henniker. No other house had such panelling, such square fine rooms, such a sweep of woods and fields and sky, as showed through the handsome twenty-four paned windows at Ocean Born Mary's.

And certainly, no other house had a solid 8 x 3 foot hearthstone in front of the big kitchen fireplace—a hearthstone with a hole drilled through it, so it could be hoisted up and used to make the cover of a very solid coffin.

"When I die I want you to bury me there," said Don Pedro to Mary Wallace.

But they didn't often think of death. The children grew up happily in the big, beautifully furnished house, and their mother was the pride of the countryside, driving about in the coach and four the mysterious old man had given her.

Some ten years after Ocean Born Mary came to live in his black house, Don Pedro took a trip to the sea-coast. When he came back he had with him a heavy sea chest which he buried outside the house that very night. His seaman who was so handy with the knife stood by to help him. Ocean Born Mary heard the sound of earth being shovelled and the curses of the men as they lowered the heavy chest into the ground. Then there was another sound, like a dull blow, and a groan, and the thud of earth being piled on earth. No one ever saw the seaman again, and they all knew better than to ask what had happened.

The Wallace boys grew up and went out into their own lives, but Ocean Born Mary stayed at the black house. One day, when she came back from her drive, she found the place deserted. The slaves were cowering in the shed and Don Pedro lay in the orchard, a sailor's cutlass sticking out between his shoulder blades. Ocean Born Mary had him buried as he had directed, under the hearth slab in the kitchen. And still she stayed on, in the house where she had never had to be afraid.

She was ninety-four when she died, and then the house stood empty. But the country people who admired it so much still kept away. There were some who thought they saw lights in the empty rooms. Horses, others said, stumbled and shied on the road where Ocean Born Mary had driven with her coach and four. A curious farmer, peering through one of the small paned windows at dusk, saw, in one terrifying flash, a tall woman's figure "floating" on the stairs.

Many people, including Mrs. Roy, the present owner, and her son, think some sort of guardian power surrounds the house. Once, when it had stood deserted for years, boys set a mattress on fire and tried to burn the place down. But the fire was seen and stopped by a man who had just "felt like" taking a walk up the mountain road that evening. Several people have tried living there, but no one stays long unless he has pride and responsibility about keeping things as nearly as he can the way they were in Ocean Born Mary's day.

" 'She' would never have left us in peace here so long," say the Roys, "if we hadn't always tried to do our best by her house."

They make no claim of having entirely to themselves

the property that stands in their name. They talk and think of Ocean Born Mary and the pirate captain as though they were near them most of the time. "Here at Ocean Born Mary's," they say; not, "here at our house."

Mrs. Roy has heard footsteps often coming up the stairs, and she takes it for granted there is a third presence in her house where she lives with her son—a tall woman in white whom she is quite used to seeing.

People with psychic powers feel impelled toward the grim hearthstone in the old kitchen; and they all agree there's something of great value hidden near the house.

One medium "got in touch" with Captain Pedro and told him she wanted to know where the treasure was hidden, so the present owner could have it.

"I buried it. Let her find it," was all the answer she could get.

Another medium, a man who practices the old country arts of herb healing, visited the house.

"We were up there several times," writes his wife, "and my husband, after hearing the story, tried to see what he could get. . . . He was very strong in getting impressions on a material subject. He got some very strong ones there."

Unfortunately, she goes on to say,

"None of them as far as we know have yet materialized, so it would not be advisable to put them in a printed book. They may later materialize. I don't say they won't. I know by experience that you have to give spirits their own time. You can't demand of them."

Ocean Born Mary's "presence," the groans of Don Pedro, the psychic's sense of buried treasure—it's a strange atmosphere for a house in the New Hampshire woods, an atmosphere built into it by a desperate man who hasn't been forgotten yet, although his house has been old now for a hundred and fifty years.

Fiddler, Play Fast, Play Faster

By RUTH SAWYER

It is a strange island and an enchanted one—our Isle of Man. It took many a thousand years and more before mankind discovered it, it being well-known that the spirits of water, of earth, of air and fire did put on it an enchantment, hiding it with a blue flame of mist, so that it could not be seen by mortal eye. The mist was made out of the heat of a great fire and the salt vapor of the sea and it covered the island like a bank of clouds. Then one day the fire was let out, the sea grew quiet, and lo, the island stood out in all its height of mountains and ruggedness of coast, its green of fens and rushing of waterfalls. Sailors passing saw it. And from that day forth men came to it and much of its enchantment was lost.

But not all. Let you know that at all seasons of the year there are spirits abroad on the Isle, working their charms and making their mischief. And there is on the coast, overhanging the sea, a great cavern reaching below the earth, out of which the Devil comes when it

This story is from The Long Christmas *by Ruth Sawyer*

pleases him, to walk where he will upon the Isle. A wise Manxman does not go far without a scrap of iron or a lump of salt in his pocket; and if it is night, likely, he will have stuck in his cap a sprig of rowan and a sprig of wormwood, feather from a seagull's wing and skin from a conger eel. For these keep away evil spirits; and who upon the Isle would meet with evil, or who would give himself foolishly into its power?

So it is that in the south upon the ramparts of Castle

97

Rushen the cannon are mounted on stone crosses above the ramparts; and when a south Manxman knocks at his neighbor's door he does not cry out: "Are you within?" But rather he asks: "Are there any sinners inside?" For evil is a fearsome thing, and who would have traffic with it?

I am long beginning my tale, but some there may be who know little of our Isle and a storyteller cannot always bring his listeners by the straightest road to the story he has to tell. This one is of the south, where the mists hang the heaviest, where the huts are built of turf and thatched with broom, where the cattle are small and the goats many, and where a farmer will tell you he has had his herd brought to fold by the fenodyree—a goblin that is half goat, half boy. But that is another tale.

Let me begin with an old Manx saying—it tunes the story well: "When a poor man helps another, God in His Heaven laughs with delight." This shows you that the men of Man are kind to one another, and God is not far from them even when the Devil walks abroad.

Count a hundred years, and as many more as you like, and you will come to the time of my story. Beyond Castletown in the sheading of Kirk Christ Rushen lived, then, a lump of a lad named Billy Nell Kewley. He could draw as sweet music from the fiddle as any fiddler of Man. When the Christmas-time began, he was first abroad with his fiddle. Up the glens and over the fens, fiddling for this neighbor and that as the night ran out, calling the hour and crying the weather, that those snug on their beds of chaff would know before the day broke what kind of day it would be making. Before Yule he started his fiddling, playing half out of the night and half into the day, playing this and playing that, carrying with him, carefully in his cap, the sprig of rowan and the sprig of wormwood, with the iron and salt in the pocket of his brown woolen breeches. And there you have Billy Nell Kewley on the Eve of Saint Fingan.

Now over Castletown on a high building of cliff rises Castle Rushen. Beyond stands the oldest monastery on the Isle, in ruin these hundreds of years, Rushen Abbey, with its hundred treens of land. It was through the Forest of Rushen Billy Nell was coming on Saint Thomas's Eve, down the Glen to the Quiggan hut, playing the tune "Andisop" and whistling a running of notes to go with it. He broke the whistle, ready to call the hour: "Two of the morning," and the weather: "Cold—with a mist over all," when he heard the running of feet behind him in the dark.

Quick as a falcon he reached for the sprig in his cap. It was gone; the pushing through the green boughs of the forest had torn it. He quickened his own feet. Could it be a buggan after him—an ugly, evil one, a fiend of Man who cursed mortals and bore malice against them, who would bring a body to perdition and then laugh at him? Billy Nell's feet went fast—went faster.

But his ear, dropping behind him, picked up the

99

sound of other feet; they were going fast—and faster. Could it be the fenodyree—the hairy one? That would be not so terrible. The fenodyree played pranks, but he, having once loved a human maid, did not bring evil to humans. And he lived, if the ancient ones could be believed, in Glen Rushen.

And then a voice spoke out of the blackness. "Stop, I command!"

What power lay in that voice! It brought the feet of Billy Nell to a stop—for all he wanted them to go on, expected them to keep running. Afterwards he was remembering the salt and iron in his pocket he might have thrown between himself and what followed so closely after him out of the mist. But he did nothing but stop—stop and say to himself: "Billy Nell Kewley, could it be the Noid ny Hanmey who commands—the Enemy of the Soul?" And he stood stock still in the darkness too frightened to shiver, for it was the Devil himself he was thinking of.

He who spoke appeared, carrying with him a kind of reddish light that came from everywhere and nowhere, a light the color of fever, or heat lightning, or of the very pit of Hell. But when Billy Nell looked he saw as fine a gentleman as ever had come to Man— fine and tall, grave and stern, well clothed in knee breeches and silver buckles and lace and such finery. He spoke with grace and grimness: "Billy Nell Kewley of Castletown, I have heard you are a monstrous good fiddler. No one better, so they say."

"I play fair, sir," said Billy Nell modestly.

"I would have you play for me. Look!" He dipped into a pocket of his breeches and drawing out a hand so white, so tapering, it might have been a lady's, he showed Billy Nell gold pieces. And in the reddish light that came from everywhere and nowhere Billy saw the strange marking on them. "You shall have as many of these as you can carry away with you if you will fiddle for me and my company three nights from tonight," said the fine one.

"And where shall I fiddle?" asked Billy Nell Kewley.

"I will send a messenger for you, Billy Nell; half-way up the Glen he will meet you. This side of midnight he will meet you."

"I will come," said the fiddler, for he had never heard of so much gold—to be his for a night's fiddling. And being not half so fearful he began to shiver. At that moment a cock crew far away, a bough brushed his eyes, the mist hung about him like a cloak, and he was alone. Then he ran, ran to Quiggan's hut, calling the hour: "Three of the clock," crying the weather: "Cold with a heavy mist."

The next day he counted, did Billy Nell Kewley, counted the days up to three and found that the night he was to fiddle for all the gold he could carry with him was Christmas Eve. A kind of terror took hold of him. What manner of spirit was the Enemy of the Soul? Could he be anything he chose to be—a devil in Hell or a fine gentleman on Earth? He ran about asking everyone, and everyone gave him a different answer. He went to the monks of the Abbey and found them working in their gardens, their black cowls thrown back from their faces, their bare feet treading the brown earth.

The Abbott came, and dour enough he looked. "Shall I go, your reverence? Shall I fiddle for one I know not? Is it good gold he is giving me?" asked Billy Nell.

"I cannot answer any one of those questions," said the Abbott. "That night alone can give the answers: Is the gold good or cursed? Is the man noble or is he the Devil? But go. Carry salt, carry iron and bollan bane. Play a dance and watch. Play another—and watch. Then play a Christmas hymn and see!"

This side of midnight, Christmas Eve, Billy Nell Kewley climbed the Glen, his fiddle wrapped in a lamb's fleece to keep out the wet. Mist, now blue, now red, hung over the blackness, so thick he had to feel his way along the track with his feet, stumbling.

He passed where Castle Rushen should have stood. He passed on, was caught up and carried as by the mist and in it. He felt his feet leave the track, he felt them gain it again. And then the mist rolled back like clouds after a storm and before him he saw such a splendid sight as no lump of a lad had ever beheld before. A castle, with courtyard and corridors, with piazzas and high roofings, spread before him all a-glowing with light. Windows wide and doorways wide, and streaming with the light came laughter. And there was his host more splendid than all, with velvet and satin, silver and jewels. About him moved what Billy Nell took to be highborn lords and ladies, come from overseas no doubt, for never had he seen their like on Man.

In the middle of the great hall he stood, unwrapping his fiddle, sweetening the strings, rosining the bow, limbering his fingers. The laughter died. His host shouted:

"Fiddler, play fast—play faster!"

In all his life and never again did Billy Nell play as he played that night. The music of his fiddle made the music of a hundred fiddles. About him whirled the dancers like crazy rainbows: blue and orange, purple and yellow, green and red all mixed together until his head swam with the color. And yet the sound of the dancers' feet was the sound of the grass growing or the corn ripening or the holly reddening—which is to say no sound at all. Only there was the sound of his playing, and above that the sound of his host shouting, always shouting:

"Fiddler, play fast—play faster!"

Ever faster—ever faster! It was as with a mighty wind Billy Nell played now, drawing the wild, mad music from his fiddle. He played tunes he had never heard before, tunes which cried and shrieked and howled and sighed and sobbed and cried out in pain.

"Play fast—play faster!"

He saw one standing by the door—a monk in a black cowl, barefooted, a monk who looked at him with deep, sad eyes and held two fingers of his hand to his lips as if to hush the music.

Then, and not till then, did Billy Nell Kewley remember what the Abbott had told him. But the monk —how came he here? And then he remembered that, too. A tale so old it had grown ragged with the telling, so that only a scrap here and there was left: how long ago, on the blessed Christmas Eve, a monk had slept through the Midnight Mass to the Virgin and to the new-born Child, and how, at complin on Christmas Day, he was missing and never seen again. The ancient ones said that the Devil had taken him away, that Enemy of All Souls, had stolen his soul because he had slept over Mass.

Terror left Billy Nell. He swept his bow so fast over the strings of his fiddle that his eyes could not follow it.

"Fiddler, play fast—play faster!"

"Master, I play faster and faster!" He moved his own body to the mad music, moved it across the hall to the door where stood the monk. He crashed out the last notes; on the floor at the feet of the monk he dropped iron, salt, and bollan bane. Then out of the silence he drew the notes of a Christmas carol—softly, sweetly it rose on the air:

> Adeste fideles, laeti triumphantes,
> Venite, venite in Bethlehem:
> Natum videte, Regem angelorum:
> Venite adoremus, venite adoremus,
> Venite adoremus—Dominum.

Racked were the ears of Billy Nell at the sounds which surged above the music, groans and wailing, the agony of souls damned. Racked were his eyes with the sights he saw: the servants turned to fleshless skeletons, the lords and ladies to howling demons. And the monk with the black cowl and bare feet sifted down to the grass beneath the vanishing castle—a heap of gray dust. But in the dust shone one small spark of holy light— a monk's soul, freed. And Billy Nell took it in his hand and tossed it high in the wind as one tosses a falcon to to the sky for free passage. And he watched it go its skimming way until the sky gathered it in.

Billy Nell Kewley played his way down the Glen, stopping to call the hour: "Three of this blessed Christmas Morning," stopping to cry the weather: "The sky is clear . . . the Christ is born."

The Water Ghost
of Harrowby Hall

By JOHN KENDRICK BANGS

The trouble with Harrowby Hall was that it was haunted, and, what was worse, the ghost did not content itself with merely appearing at the bedside of the afflicted person who saw it, but persisted in remaining there for one mortal hour before it would disappear.

It never appeared except on Christmas Eve, and then as the clock was striking twelve, in which respect alone was it lacking in that originality which in these days is a *sine qua non* of success in spectral life. The owners of Harrowby Hall had done their utmost to rid themselves of the damp and dewy lady who rose up out of the best bedroom floor at midnight, but without avail. They had tried stopping the clock, so that the ghost would not know when it was midnight; but she made her appearance just the same, with that fearful miasmatic personality of hers, and there she would stand

This story is from The Water Ghost and Others *by John Kendrick Bangs*

until everything about her was thoroughly saturated.

Then the owners of Harrowby Hall calked up every crack in the floor with the very best quality of hemp, and over this were placed layers of tar and canvas; the walls were made waterproof, and the doors and windows likewise, the proprietors having conceived the notion that the unexorcised lady would find it difficult to leak into the room after these precautions had been taken; but even this did not suffice. The following Christmas Eve she appeared as promptly as before, and frightened the occupant of the room quite out of his senses by sitting down alongside of him and gazing with her cavernous blue eyes into his; and he noticed, too, that in her long, aqueously bony fingers bits of dripping seaweed were entwined, the ends hanging down, and these ends she drew across his forehead until he became like one insane. And then he swooned away, and was found unconscious in his bed the next morning by his host, simply saturated with sea-water and fright, from the combined effects of which he never recovered, dying four years later of pneumonia and nervous prostration at the age of seventy-eight.

The next year the master of Harrowby Hall decided not to have the best spare bedroom opened at all, thinking that perhaps the ghost's thirst for making herself disagreeable would be satisfied by haunting the furniture, but the plan was as unavailing as the many that had preceded it.

The ghost appeared as usual in the room—that is, it

was supposed she did, for the hangings were dripping wet the next morning, and in the parlor below the haunted room a great damp spot appeared on the ceiling. Finding no one there, she immediately set out to learn the reason why, and she chose none other to haunt than the owner of Harrowby himself. She found him in his own cosy room drinking whiskey—whiskey undiluted—and felicitating himself upon having foiled her ghostship, when all of a sudden the curl went out of his hair, his whiskey bottle filled and overflowed, and he was himself in a condition similar to that of a man who has fallen into a water-butt. When he recovered from the shock, which was a painful one, he saw before him the lady of the cavernous eyes and seaweed fingers. The sight was so unexpected and so terrifying that he fainted, but immediately came to, because of the vast amount of water in his hair, which, trickling down over his face, restored his consciousness.

Now it so happened that the master of Harrowby was a brave man, and while he was not particularly fond of interviewing ghosts, especially such quenching ghosts as the one before him, he was not to be daunted by an apparition. He had paid the lady the compliment of fainting from the effects of his first surprise, and now that he had come to he intended to find out a few things he felt he had a right to know. He would have liked to put on a dry suit of clothes first, but the apparition declined to leave him for an instant until her hour was up, and he was forced to deny himself that pleasure.

Every time he would move she would follow him, with the result that everything she came in contact with got a ducking. In an effort to warm himself up he approached the fire, an unfortunate move as it turned out, because it brought the ghost directly over the fire, which immediately was extinguished. The whiskey became utterly valueless as a comforter to his chilled system, because it was by this time diluted to a proportion of ninety per cent of water. The only thing he could do to ward off the evil effects of his encounter he did, and that was to swallow ten two-grain quinine pills, which he managed to put into his mouth before the ghost had time to interfere. Having done this, he turned with some asperity to the ghost, and said:

"Far be it from me to be impolite to a woman, madam, but I'm hanged if it wouldn't please me better if you'd stop these infernal visits of yours to this house. Go sit out on the lake, if you like that sort of thing; soak the water-butt, if you wish; but do not, I implore you, come into a gentleman's house and saturate him and his possessions in this way. It is damned disagreeable."

"Henry Hartwick Oglethorpe," said the ghost, in a gurgling voice, "you don't know what you are talking about."

"Madam," returned the unhappy householder, "I wish that remark were strictly truthful. I was talking about you. It would be shillings and pence—nay, pounds, in my pocket, madam, if I did not know you."

The sight was so unexpected and so terrifying that he fainted . . .

"That is a bit of specious nonsense," returned the ghost, throwing a quart of indignation into the face of the master of Harrowby. "It may rank high as repartee, but as a comment upon my statement, that you do not know what you are talking about, it savors of irrelevant impertinence. You do not know that I am compelled to haunt this place year after year by inexorable fate. It is no pleasure to me to enter this house, and ruin and mildew everything I touch. I never aspired to be a shower-bath, but it is my doom. Do you know who I am?"

"No, I don't," returned the master of Harrowby. "I should say you were the Lady of the Lake, or Little Sallie Waters."

"You are a witty man for your years," said the ghost.

"Well, my humor is drier than yours ever will be," returned the master.

"No doubt. I'm never dry. I am the Water Ghost of Harrowby Hall, and dryness is a quality entirely beyond my wildest hope. I have been the incumbent of this highly unpleasant office for two hundred years to-night."

"How the deuce did you ever come to get elected?" asked the master.

"Through a suicide," replied the specter. "I am the ghost of that fair maiden whose picture hangs over the mantelpiece in the drawing-room. I should have been your great-great-great-great-great-aunt if I had lived, Henry Hartwick Oglethorpe, for I was the own sister of your great-great-great-great-great-grandfather."

"But what induced you to get this house into such a predicament?"

"I was not to blame, sir," returned the lady. "It was my father's fault. He it was who built Harrowby Hall, and the haunted chamber was to have been mine. My father had it furnished in pink and yellow, knowing well that blue and gray formed the only combination of color I could tolerate. He did it merely to spite me, and, with what I deem a proper spirit, I declined to live in the room; whereupon my father said I could live there or on the lawn, he didn't care which. That night I ran from the house and jumped over the cliff into the sea."

"That was rash," said the master of Harrowby. "So I've heard," returned the ghost. "If I had known what the consequences were to be I should not have jumped; but I really never realized what I was doing until after I was drowned. I had been drowned a week when a sea-nymph came to me and informed me that I was to be one of her followers forever afterwards, adding that it should be my doom to haunt Harrowby Hall for one hour every Christmas Eve throughout the rest of eternity. I was to haunt that room on such Christmas Eves as I found it inhabited; and if it should turn out not to be inhabited, I was and am to spend the allotted hour with the head of the house."

"I'll sell the place."

"That you cannot do, for it is also required of me that I shall appear as the deeds are to be delivered to any purchaser, and divulge to him the awful secret of the house."

"Do you mean to tell me that on every Christmas Eve that I don't happen to have somebody in that guest-chamber, you are going to haunt me wherever I may be, ruining my whiskey, taking all the curl out of my hair, extinguishing my fire, and soaking me through to the skin?" demanded the master.

"You have stated the case, Oglethorpe. And what is more," said the water ghost, "it doesn't make the slightest difference where you are, if I find that room empty, wherever you may be I shall douse you with my spectral pres—"

Here the clock struck one, and immediately the apparition faded away. It was perhaps more of a trickle than a fade, but as a disappearance it was complete.

"By St. George and his Dragon!" ejaculated the master of Harrowby, wringing his hands. "It is guineas to hot-cross buns that next Christmas there's an occupant of the spare room, or I spend the night in a bathtub."

But the master of Harrowby would have lost his wager had there been anyone there to take him up, for when Christmas Eve came again he was in his grave, never having recovered from the cold contracted that awful night. Harrowby Hall was closed, and the heir to the estate was in London, where to him in his chambers came the same experience that his father had gone

113

through, saving only that, being younger and stronger, he survived the shock. Everything in his rooms was ruined—his clocks were rusted in the works; a fine collection of water-color drawings was entirely obliterated by the onslaught of the water ghost; and what was worse, the apartments below his were drenched with the water soaking through the floors, a damage for which he was compelled to pay, and which resulted in his being requested by his landlady to vacate the premises immediately.

The story of the visitation inflicted upon his family had gone abroad, and no one could be got to invite him out to any function save afternoon teas and receptions. Fathers of daughters declined to permit him to remain in their houses later than eight o'clock at night, not knowing but that some emergency might arise in the supernatural world which would require the unexpected appearance of the water ghost in this on nights other than Christmas Eve, and before the mystic hour when weary churchyards, ignoring the rules which are supposed to govern polite society, begin to yawn. Nor would maids themselves have aught to do with him, fearing the destruction by the sudden incursion of aqueous femininity of the costumes which they held most dear.

So the heir of Harrowby Hall resolved, as his ancestors for several generations before him had resolved, that something must be done. His first thought was to make one of his servants occupy the haunted room at the crucial moment; but in this he failed, because the servants themselves knew the history of that room and rebelled. None of his friends would consent to sacrifice their personal comfort to his, nor was there to be found in all England a man so poor as to be willing to occupy the doomed chamber on Christmas Eve for pay.

Then the thought came to the heir to have the fireplace in the room enlarged, so that he might evaporate the ghost at its first appearance, and he was felicitating himself upon the ingenuity of his plan, when he remembered what his father had told him—how that no fire could withstand the lady's extremely contagious dampness. And then he bethought him of steam-pipes. These, he remembered, could lie hundreds of feet deep in water, and still retain sufficient heat to drive the water away in vapor; and as a result of this thought the haunted room was heated by steam to a withering degree, and the heir for six months attended daily the Turkish baths, so that when Christmas Eve came he could himself withstand the awful temperature of the room.

The scheme was only partially successful. The water ghost appeared at the specified time, and found the heir of Harrowby prepared; but hot as the room was, it shortened her visit by no more than five minutes in the hour, during which time the nervous system of the young master was well-nigh shattered, and the room itself was cracked and warped to an extent which required the outlay of a large sum of money to remedy.

And worse than this, as the last drop of the water ghost was slowly sizzling itself out on the floor, she whispered to her would-be conqueror that his scheme would avail him nothing, because there was still water in great plenty where she came from, and that next year would find her rehabilitated and as exasperatingly saturating as ever.

It was then that the natural action of the mind, in going from one extreme to the other, suggested to the ingenious heir of Harrowby the means by which the water ghost was ultimately conquered, and happiness once more came within the grasp of the house of Oglethorpe.

The heir provided himself with a warm suit of fur underclothing. Donning this with the furry side in, he placed over it a rubber garment, tightfitting, which he wore just as a woman wears a jersey. On top of this he placed another set of underclothing, this suit made of wool, and over this was a second rubber garment like the first. Upon his head he placed a light and comfortable diving helmet, and so clad, on the following Christmas Eve he awaited the coming of his tormentor.

It was a bitterly cold night that brought to a close this twenty-fourth day of December. The air outside was still, but the temperature was below zero. Within all was quiet, the servants of Harrowby Hall awaiting with beating hearts the outcome of their master's campaign against his supernatural visitor.

The master himself was lying on the bed in the

haunted room, clad as has already been indicated, and then—

The clock clanged out the hour of twelve.

There was a sudden banging of doors, a blast of cold air swept through the halls, the door leading into the haunted chamber flew open, a splash was heard, and the water ghost was seen standing at the side of the heir of Harrowby, from whose outer dress there streamed rivulets of water, but whose own person deep down under the various garments he wore was as dry and as warm as he could have wished.

"Ha!" said the young master of Harrowby. "I'm glad to see you."

"You are the most original man I've met, if that is true," returned the ghost. "May I ask where did you get that hat?"

"Certainly, madam," returned the master, courteously. "It is a little portable observatory I had made for just such emergencies as this. But, tell me, is it true that you are doomed to follow me about for one mortal hour—to stand where I stand, to sit where I sit?"

"That is my delectable fate," returned the lady.

"We'll go out on the lake," said the master, starting up.

"You can't get rid of me that way," returned the ghost. "The water won't swallow me up; in fact, it will just add to my present bulk."

"Nevertheless," said the master, firmly, "we will go out on the lake."

"But my dear sir," returned the ghost, with a pale reluctance, "it is fearfully cold out there. You will be frozen hard before you've been out ten minutes."

"Oh, no, I'll not," replied the master. "I am very warmly dressed. Come!" This last in a tone of command that made the ghost ripple.

And they started.

They had not gone far before the water ghost showed signs of distress.

"You walk too slowly," she said. "I am nearly frozen. My knees are so stiff now I can hardly move. I beseech you to accelerate your step."

"I should like to oblige a lady," returned the master, courteously, "but my clothes are rather heavy, and a hundred yards an hour is about my speed. Indeed, I think we would better sit down here on this snowdrift, and talk matters over."

"Do not! Do not do so, I beg!" cried the ghost. "Let me move on. I feel myself growing rigid as it is. If we stop here, I shall be frozen stiff."

"That, madam," said the master slowly, and seating himself on an ice-cake—"that is why I have brought you here. We have been on this spot just ten minutes; we have fifty more. Take your time about it, madam, but freeze, that is all I ask of you."

"I cannot move my right leg now," cried the ghost, in despair, "and my overskirt is a solid sheet of ice. Oh, good, kind Mr. Oglethorpe, light a fire, and let me go free from these icy fetters."

"Never, madam. It cannot be. I have you at last."

"Alas!" cried the ghost, a tear trickling down her frozen cheek. "Help me, I beg. I congeal!"

"Congeal, madam, congeal!" returned Oglethorpe, coldly. "You have drenched me and mine for two hundred and three years, madam. Tonight, you have had your last drench."

"Ah, but I shall thaw out again, and then you'll see. Instead of the comfortably tepid, genial ghost I have been in my past, sir, I shall be iced-water," cried the lady, threateningly.

"No, you won't either," returned Oglethorpe; "for when you are frozen quite stiff, I shall send you to a cold-storage warehouse, and there shall you remain an icy work of art forever more."

"But warehouses burn."

"So they do, but this warehouse cannot burn. It is made of asbestos and surrounding it are fireproof walls, and within those walls the temperature is now and shall forever be 416 degrees below the zero point; low enough to make an icicle of any flame in this world—or the next," the master added, with an ill-suppressed chuckle.

"For the last time let me beseech you. I would go on my knees to you, Oglethorpe, were they not already frozen. I beg of you do not doo—"

Here even the words froze on the water ghost's lips and the clock struck one. There was a momentary tremor throughout the ice-bound form, and the moon, coming out from behind a cloud, shone down on the rigid figure of a beautiful woman sculptured in clear, transparent ice. There stood the ghost of Harrowby Hall, conquered by the cold, a prisoner for all time.

The heir of Harrowby had won at last, and today in a large storage house in London stands the frigid form of one who will never again flood the house of Oglethorpe with woe and sea-water.

As for the heir of Harrowby, his success in coping with a ghost has made him famous, a fame that still lingers about him, although his victory took place some twenty years ago; and so far from being unpopular with the fair sex, as he was when we first knew him, he has not only been married twice, but is to lead a third bride to the altar before the year is out.

The Golden Pitcher

By BERTHA L. GUNTERMAN

The province of Soria is, next to that of Granada, most famous in Spain for picturesque legends. It is one of the smallest and most arid provinces of the Peninsula, and the climate is the coldest imaginable in the sunny south. Chains of picturesque mountains encircle deep valleys.

In certain parts the vegetation is strong and rich, with here and there great stretches of pine and oak forest. In other parts lie immense pasture grounds, formerly overspread by flocks of sheep. But the greater part of the country shows nothing but bare mountains covered with snow for most of the year.

Huge masses of granite tower above on each side of the pathway; here and there deep ravines and cascades supply the springs, in which the water is supposed to be extraordinarily good. The children living near these springs are employed to carry the water for household use because there is a saying among the country people

This story is from Castles in Spain and Other Enchantments by Bertha L. Gunterman

121

that those little ones who are best and purest will one day come upon a hidden Treasure in the mountain.

Carmenita was the daughter of Miguel Todega, a well-to-do farmer of Soria; her mother had died when she was born. Miguel Todega had married, to please himself, a kind and good woman, but so poor that he had disappointed his ambitious old mother. Miguel's mother died soon after her daughter-in-law, and Carmenita was brought up by an aunt who disliked her for she not only resembled her gentle mother in mind and spirit, but also in face and figure.

One would have thought that a little baby like that would have softened a heart even of stone. But Juana Todega had no heart, and she said she had no time for sentimentality. She had worked hard in her youth, and she intended that Carmenita should do the same. She was a grasping, mischievous, hard-featured woman. with a bad temper and a sharp tongue, and all little Carmenita's mistakes were harshly punished.

If Miguel Todega had been much at home he would have seen how his child was ill-treated, but he was constantly absent on business, and Carmenita never complained. She adored her father, who loved her passionately, not only because she was his only daughter, but more because she resembled so much his beloved Carmen, the love of his youth, whom he had lost.

The little girl obeyed her aunt and did her work well; but she sometimes looked so weary and pitiful that it was plain her tasks were beyond her strength.

But as she never murmured nor showed any temper, people thought that all was well in that household.

Every morning and evening the aunt sent Carmenita with two heavy copper jars to a spring about half a mile from the house. There a large black mountain reared its huge mass behind the little spring in the valley, which was fed by the cascades and mountain torrents. The mountain was called by the peasants *El Diablo* because it was so dark and forbidding.

The curious cap El Diablo wore whenever a storm was coming on and the strange, uncanny noises constantly heard near it after dark made almost everyone fear to go to this spring after nightfall. But Juana Todega scorned the superstitious idea and insisted that little Carmenita go to the spring for water.

And though the child was sometimes awed by the grandeur and loneliness of the nearby mountains, she preferred them to staying at home to be scolded and beaten by her aunt.

Carmenita was a great favorite with the other children of the village, and when sometimes she had a little leisure from her dreary tasks, she was always as welcome as the flowers. But there were days when her aunt was unusually severe, and unable to bear the misery heaped upon her, Carmenita would take her bit of knitting and retire to the spring of El Diablo to think over her troubles, and calm her wounded spirit.

She had often heard the curious story of hidden Treasure in the mountains around the Soria, but she never thought much about finding it, because she felt sure that she was not good enough for such fortune.

Her father's homecoming was always a great delight to Carmenita, for besides the pleasure of being with him, Juana Todega was then more merciful to her. The aunt knew from experience how angry Miguel could be if he were roused, and she did not dare scold or mistreat his daughter before his very eyes. So Carmenita always had a respite from her aunt's tongue and evil temper while her father remained at home.

And so the years passed until Carmenita was seventeen. She was very like her mother, and sometimes her father sighed sadly as he looked at her. Graceful and slender with sweet, deep, gray eyes and a fresh, clear voice, she made many a man's heart turn within him, as she passed on her way to El Diablo with her waterjars, and answered all greeting with her sunny smile and a pleasant word.

It was St. John's Eve, and there was to be a dance on the village green at the close of day. Carmenita danced well, with a step as light as a fairy's; and all the youths of the neighborhood vied with one another in securing her as a partner. She enjoyed fete-days, when she was free from drudgery, and could unbend in enjoyment and delight, sure that her aunt would not be near with her usual scolding and fault-finding.

Dona Juana did not approve of anything like holiday-making. In her day, she used to say, no one thought of dancing and frolicking about like lambs and goats.

When she was young, a quiet walk and mass in the morning, and a few friends to chat with in the evening, was all the fete that was necessary for a young, well-conducted girl.

So she always refused to accompany Carmenita to these little merry-makings, but sent her in care of a neighbor, an elderly and respectable peasant woman, with daughters of her own. The neighbor was nothing loath, for her son Carlos was much taken with Carmenita's charms, and everyone said that they would make a match of it. In truth they were a handsome pair, and no one said anything but good of either of them. Therefore old Dona Ursula considered Carmenita as another daughter, and was, if possible, prouder of her than of her own girls.

On this particular St. John's Eve, Carmenita dressed herself with special care. This was the last fete before her father returned, when her betrothal to Carlos would be celebrated. She knew that she should be with Carlos there, and she felt pride in making herself as pretty as she could, knowing that he would be so proud of her. Just as she was ready to start for Dona Ursula's house, Aunt Juana called to her, and said:

"We have not a drop of water in the house. It is not yet dark, and there will be plenty of time to go for the water and return, as there will be no dancing for an hour or more."

Carmenita could scarcely keep back the tears as she listened to her aunt's words.

"Is it absolutely necessary for me to go, Aunt Juana?" she said. "I have put on my best clothes, and I shall get them wet at the spring."

"You never have been splashed before, and if you are careful you need not be now," was Juana's answer. "But have the water we must; for it is hot weather."

"For once could you not get it yourself?" pleaded Carmenita. "Carlos will be waiting for me at the Plaza."

Whereupon Juana burst out in a torrent of abuse. For a moment Carmenita stood speechless, as though she had been stunned. From childhood she had been accustomed to her aunt's unseemly language, and she did not mind so much the words she used. But the disappointment was very great, almost more than she could bear. Her eyes filled with tears, and she kept them from brimming over only by sheer force of will.

Without another word she took up the water-jars and started to the spring. Dona Ursula lived at the other end of the village from her, so that she could not stop and tell her that she would be late. But she hoped, if she hurried, to reach the Plaza in time to keep her appointment with Carlos.

But the hours slipped by, and Carmenita did not return. Dona Ursula and her daughters waited until the daylight faded away, and the stars cames out one by one. But still no Carmenita. At last they could wait no longer, and went on to the Plaza, thinking that perhaps she would be there. But she was nowhere to be seen, and Carlos wandered about sadly searching among the many groups of peasants who had come for the dancing.

At first he was angry thinking that Carmenita had deceived him; but as the evening faded into night he became alarmed, and went to Miguel Todega's house in the hope of finding her. But there instead he found Juana, frightened nearly out of her wits and walking up and down the kitchen, wringing her hands and tearing her hair.

"Oh, Carlos, I cannot find her!" cried she, when she saw him standing in the doorway. "I was cruel and cross, and, although she begged to go to the dance in the Plaza, I sent her to fetch water at El Diablo. She went without a murmur, although I know that she thought me hard.

"When an hour had passed and she did not return, I was fearful of what I had done, and went to look for her. Even on bright days, as you know, El Diablo is not a cheerful place, and the loneliness and desolation along the road is awful. When I got to the spring, I found the jars beside it on the brink, but no Carmenita. I called and called and walked up and down, shrieking her name with all my might. No one could I see, and not a sound did I hear.

"Then all of a sudden I heard the tramp of horses' feet, and looking in the direction of the sound I saw a procession of horses mounted by still, pale men, who turned their heads neither to the right nor the left, but continued straight along in a stately march on the high-road. They wore curious, twisted handkerchiefs on their heads, and were not dressed like anyone I ever saw before. They did not see me, for I was hidden behind a rock.

"After they had passed, I called and called to Carmenita, but she did not answer so I came home again. If those ghostly-looking men have seen her, no one knows what her fate may be. And it is all my fault. What shall I say to Miguel when he returns?—I, who have been the cause of harm to Carmenita!"

And she sobbed and cried and wrung her hands as if no one were present.

Carlos had listened to Juana's long speech with wonderment. It was the longest he had ever heard her make, for she was singularly silent with her neighbors. But when she mentioned the procession of ghostly people she had seen, his cheek turned pale and he staggered into a chair. He remembered that this was the Eve of St. John, the night when all Moors, wherever buried, rise from their resting-places and go to do homage to their king in Granada. What if they had taken Carmenita along with them?

For some time he stared at Juana in silence, but at last his anger overcame him, and he overwhelmed her with reproaches.

"Accursed woman!" he cried, "you have been the torment and slave-driver of my poor girl. All her life you have made her miserable when her father was not near to see how you treated her. And now, on this night, when you knew, as all Spaniards do know, that the spirits of the dead are free to go about the earth as on the night of All Hallowe'en, you forced her to go to the spring of El Diablo because you grudged her innocent pleasure, in which you can take no part. If anything happens to Carmenita, I shall hold you responsible, and shall tell everyone that you are to blame for her death."

With these words he rushed out of the house, leaving Juana pale as a ghost, wringing her hands and speechless with terror.

Carlos made his way towards the spring of El Diablo. The moon was sailing through an unclouded sky. Every rock and tuft of grass was as clearly seen as if it were noontide. He looked along the road anxiously to see whether his beloved Carmenita was in sight; but not a soul could be seen along the bright, straight, dusty highway.

When he reached the spring he could see by the moonlight the water-jars which she had brought, filled to the very brim, and standing just where she had placed them ready to take home. In vain he wandered about searching for her in the defiles and paths of the mountain and calling her name. Echo alone answered him. No one appeared, and he could find no trace of his beloved Carmenita.

He searched for some hours near the dreadful mountain, and heard the tramping of horses' feet and groans all about him; but as he could see nothing, he returned home. On his way, however, he stopped and told Juana Todega of what he had heard, and of his ill-success. She seemed to be almost a mad creature and sprang at him when he entered, caught him by the wrist and shoulder and shook him, her eyes glaring at him like a she-bear deprived of her young.

"Well, have you found her? Where is she?" she cried. And when he made no answer, she shook him again. "Speak!" she shrieked. "Have you found her, or is she dead? Speak!"

Carlos was so weak from anxiety and misery that he could only shake his head, yet his expression was so fierce and angry that involuntarily Juana let go her hold of him. Frightened, she shrank back into the farthest corner of the room. But in less time than it takes to tell it, he had lifted the latch of the door and was gone.

Meanwhile Carmenita was in no danger, although she had missed the fete, and had caused all this alarm to her aunt and to her lover.

She had gone as usual to the spring of El Diablo, had filled her jars, and was preparing to return home, when she heard the sound of horses' feet. Looking up she saw a long procession of horses with riders dressed in curious costumes and trappings. They rode in solemn and stately dignity.

For a few minutes she was astonished, and looked on in childlike delight. But as the procession came near her and passed her, she suddenly felt cold and paralyzed with fear. Why, she knew not, and could not understand, but she trembled and her teeth chattered although it was a warm June evening.

But after the procession had passed she prepared to take up her jars and start for home, when she felt a hand laid on her arm. Turning round she saw a beautiful woman, with a lovely, fair face and golden hair, and the most enchanting blue eyes that she had ever beheld. The woman was very pale, and stood looking earnestly at her for several minutes after their eyes met, then at last she said in a low, sweet voice:

"I have been looking for you for a long time. Will you come and help me in a very serious matter? It will not take you long, but I have waited years for you. To you the few minutes will be nothing, but to me they will be eternity."

Carmenita was much disturbed in her mind when she heard these words, and thought to herself:

"I am fated not to go to the Plaza and dance with Carlos tonight. But if I can help this poor soul, who has waited so long for me, I have not the heart to refuse."

"Carlos can wait," replied the fair woman, answering her thoughts.

And when Carmenita started at finding her thoughts known to her companion, and turned towards her, she found the beautiful blue eyes fixed upon her, sad with the sadness of death.

"Do not refuse me," said the woman in a faint whisper, "but come with me."

And without a word Carmenita followed her, leaving the water-jars at the spring.

They walked for nearly a mile without a word, the fair woman walking ahead and Carmenita following. Where she was going, or what she was to do when she reached their destination, troubled Carmenita not at all.

She felt that she could be of use to this fair, proud woman, so strange in her manner, who knew all about Carlos, and had assured her that he could wait. That surely meant that she would be safe, and return to him in a little while. Suddenly her guide turned. The rocks opened at her touch, and she walked into a large cave, black as night.

"Shut your eyes and give me your hand," said the woman, "and rest assured that no harm of any kind shall befall you."

Carmenita felt so sure that her guide would keep her word, that without fear she shut her eyes and put her hand in that of the beautiful woman. The hand was as cold as ice, but the clasp was firm, almost like a vise, and hurt her a little. They seemed to go through several large rooms, and at last her companion stopped short.

"Open your eyes now," she said. "We are in a place where we can speak without being overheard."

Carmenita looked about her, and saw with astonishment that the walls glittered like ice, and that here and there a tinge of gold seemed mixed with it.

"Sit down here near me," said her new friend, "and

She walked into a large cave, black as night . . .

I will tell you what you can do for me. You can free me from my dreadful bondage. Centuries ago I lived. I am Moorish, and was taken prisoner by the Christians in their wars with the Moors. I learned to love my master, and cheerfully left my own people for his sake, following him to his country and repudiating my ancestors and religion.

"My father cursed me with his last breath, saying that never should I find rest for my soul till on St. John's Eve some pure maiden should kiss my lips and of her own sweet charity free my unhappy spirit. Are you willing to do this for me?

"Remember that the various forms I shall have to take will terrify you. But if you will stand by me to the end, my spirit will be liberated. Nothing can harm you, if you keep repeating your prayers. But do not for one minute stop praying or be afraid. So many have promised, but have disappointed me hitherto, that I still remain under this accursed spell.

"Take this pitcher in your left hand, hold it tightly, and do not let it go. It will bring you fortune. Do not cease your prayers for one minute, nor be frightened at anything you may hear or see. And, above all, do not answer any question, or cry out, no matter what you may see or hear. My life is in your hands, be faithful!"

Carmenita nodded her head and grasping the curious, dark pitcher in her left hand, began her prayers.

Suddenly her companion changed into a black ape,

and sat beside her. Then the cave was filled with other black apes, who chattered and grinned at her and at each other. This lasted for a few minutes; to Carmenita it seemed hours! But she grasped the pitcher tightly in her left hand, and repeated her prayers as earnestly and fervently as she could.

She tried to shut out the grinning, ugly faces, but to her horror she found that she could not close her eyes. She was obliged to see everything that happened.

Suddenly she heard the tramp of horses' feet, but she could see nothing. And every now and then there would be a call of *Mona* (monkey) followed by peals of laughter and shouts of derision. Then for a time everything was quiet, but the apes still grinned and chattered at her.

Suddenly she heard Carlos' voice calling her own name. "Carmenita, Carmenita!" it cried. "Where are you, my love? I am looking for you, and am wild with terror."

She started up eagerly but still grasping the pitcher in her left hand. In an instant more she would have answered Carlos, but she felt a hand on her arm, and turning saw the piteous and beseeching eyes of the poor ape sitting beside her. "Carlos can wait!" came into her mind; and she said her prayers out loud so that she might not hear that dear voice calling her in vain.

Again after a time all was still. She looked around and to her horror instead of a monkey's shape sitting beside her, she found that of a demon. And lo! the

135

cave was filled with demons, all dancing and laughing and jeering at her.

"Indeed, I have fallen into strange hands," was the thought that crossed her mind as she continued her prayers. Her tongue seemed tied, but she still managed to articulate, and grasped the pitcher in her left hand all the more tightly. Suddenly the little demon at her side burst into flames, and through the fire Carmenita saw her beautiful guide taking human form again.

"Kiss me on the lips now," whispered a faint voice at her side.

"*Gloria in excelsis Deo!*" cried Carmenita, as she stooped forward, and in spite of the flames she kissed the poor creature who had wandered so long under a curse. The words echoed through the cave. A sudden darkness came over Carmenita, sleep overpowered her.

When she awoke, she was lying by the spring of El Diablo, her two water-jars by her side. Grasped in her left hand was a Golden Pitcher of antique shape and exquisite Oriental workmanship.

The dawn was breaking, and the birds were beginning their morning song, when Carmenita turned her face homewards. On the road she met Carlos, dishevelled and frantic. She smiled at him, but at first he could hardly believe his eyes. Then he caught her in his arms. He kissed her, and laughed, and cried by turns.

"O, Carmenita, where have you been? The angels have been merciful and sent you back to me, for they knew that I should die without shriving if you were not with me to make me as pure and good as yourself."

Carmenita then told him all that had happened. When she showed him the Golden Pitcher, lo! it was full of gold coins. In his eagerness he put his hand into the pitcher to grasp the money and brought out pebbles! But when Carmenita put hers inside, she drew out a handful of gold pieces.

"Ah!" cried Carlos, "only the pure in heart can touch it and keep it bright. I have learned my lesson!" And he kissed Carmenita more tenderly and reverently than ever before, knowing that he had won a rare treasure for his wife.

She, dear child, wondered but said nothing. On reaching home she found her Aunt Juana in great distress of mind, wringing her hands and tearing her hair, rocking herself from side to side, wondering how she should dare to face Miguel and tell him that Carmenita was lost to them forever. There was great rejoicing, as may be imagined, when Carlos led Carmenita into the house.

In her own mind Juana Todega made splendid resolutions that she would never be unkind or cross again. The pitcher was placed in a niche where everyone could see it. Of course the whole village crowded to behold this wonderful vessel. And everyone with all his heart said that no one deserved such good fortune as did Carmenita.

Miguel's return home was still delayed. All went on in the usual way, and the adventure of El Diablo

gradually became an old story. Carmenita took her water-jars to the spring every day, and went through her
usual drudgery.

One day, when Carmenita was out at El Diablo, evil
entered into Juana's heart. She was all alone in the
house, and she thought no one would know what she
was doing. She did not know the secret of the pitcher,
but had noticed that whenever Carmenita wanted
money she put her hand in it and drew out what she
wanted. So, tempted, she went to the pitcher, which
suddenly looked dull in color, and put in her hand.

But she drew it out very quickly with a loud cry, and
found her hand covered with red ants, which had bit
and stung her sharply before she could drown them in
the pail of water. For days she went about with her hand
bound up. It was swollen to twice its usual size. But
she was warned by this experience, and never tam-
pered with Carmenita's Golden Pitcher again.

In the course of time Miguel returned to his home
and a few weeks later Carmenita and her faithful Carlos were married. They went to Barcelona to live, and
with gold from the Moor's gift Carlos bought large
silk mills there. One of the most treasured of their possessions was the Golden Pitcher, which continued to
reward Carmenita with gold whenever she was in need
of it.

Prince Godfrey Frees Mountain Dwellers and Little Shepherds from a Savage Werewolf and from Witches

By HALINA GORSKA

A short time after the disappearance of the shepherd's pet had involved Godfrey in his adventure with the elves, two other goats went astray, then a ram and four sheep, and last a large white cow, the pride of the whole herd.

The old herdsman brooded greatly over this loss and was particularly disconsolate over the cow. He was angry at the herdboys because they had a mind for nothing but pranks, he said, and could not keep their animals from harm.

When, however, shortly after that, a bull was lost, too, a bull so strong and stubborn that he would have been a match for any wolf, the old man shook his head sadly and said, "Ah, boys, 'tis some unholy power and

This story is from Prince Godfrey *by Halina Gorska*

not the wolves. As long as only goats and sheep were lost, I thought it was your carelessness that was to blame, for it is well known that they are foolish, flighty and thoughtless creatures and likely to come to grief, so that they want careful watching. But with a cow it is an altogether different matter. And what a cow, mind you. Quiet, sedate, not at all given to pranks and frolic. Still, I said to myself that even such a cow might be frightened into straying from the herd, and in the woods a mishap is easily met with. But a bull. Why, he would throw a wolf, and not the other way around."

He had scarce finished speaking when shepherds from the valley next to theirs came running and began to inquire if their neighbors had seen two cows from their own herd—one black, they said, and the other piebald.

They proceeded to complain and lament that things had been getting out of hand lately, so many cattle had disappeared under their very eyes. And not only that. Why, only yesterday two shepherds had gone into the woods to search for sheep, and had not yet returned.

Likewise, they said, farmers from near-by villages have come to us to inquire about children. It appears that they went picking berries and were lost. But, stranger yet, yesterday at evenfall there came hurrying into our valley the wife of John the Sharpshooter, who is known as the best shot of the neighborhood, and she told us, crying, that three days have gone by since he went chamois-chasing and he has not yet come home.

No doubt about it, some mighty packs of hungry and very daring wolves must have come sneaking from the other side of the mountains.

The old herdsman listened to this tale in gloomy silence, and then said, "Nay, not wolves; they are not wolves that go ravening hereabouts; it is a werewolf and his devilish crew that are stalking about. We shall all perish pitifully, we and our herds."

A great terror came over the shepherds. They all grew silent, casting fearful glances at one another. Godfrey, however, was not a whit alarmed. He began to inquire curiously about the werewolf and his crew who frightened everybody. But the old herdsman responded thus:

"It does no good talking about it. Empty talk will avail nothing and calamity is easily invited. Be on your guard. Stay close to one another. Do not scatter and God grant that we somehow come through scatheless, for an evil creature does not like a crowd." The herd-boys obeyed him and none dared leave his companions to go picking raspberries or mushrooms, while at night they huddled together like frightened sheep.

Laughter and gay talk ceased. Melancholy and fear came to reign among them. Godfrey alone did not lose his spirit, and his gay songs bore up his companions' hearts.

A few days passed in complete quiet and soon the shepherds began to take heart. Perhaps the evil was past.

First one, then another, made bold enough to stray from his companions in order to drive in a goat or to seek out some special tree for reeds.

But the wicked being did not sleep; it merely lay in wait, the better to deceive the watchful shepherds. And so it was that Jackie the Homeless, so nicknamed because he was an orphan and had no one in the world, disappeared one day without leaving a trace. He was Godfrey's dearest comrade. Dismay struck everybody, and Godfrey, despite the shepherd's interdiction, sought long and singly for his cherished companion, weeping and greatly sorrowing for him. Finally, when he returned to camp without finding the boy, he vowed in his heart he would destroy the monster. He said nothing about his decision to anyone, but constantly kept thinking of how he was going to find the werewolf.

By chance he soon found an opportunity.

One day there arrived in the valley a farmer from a far-off village in the mountains. Bowing to the herdsman, he said that he had heard of the great player from his shepherds and had come expressly to bid him to a wedding. This request did not surprise the herdsman and his boys, for, as I have said already, the fame of Godfrey's songs had spread far and wide over the region and no wedding or christening could be held without his music.

The old herdsman prided himself upon having such a player among his herders, and would gladly have given his permission. But something about this farmer did not please him; the man was shaggy like a wolf and all clothed in skins, he flashed his eyes like a wild beast, and his smile was sly and malevolent.

The old man was loath to let Godfrey go along with the stranger, therefore he took the boy aside and said, "I do not know what manner of man this is, but he has something evil in his eyes, and times are uncertain. Also, I heard my grandfather say that a werewolf can sometimes assume man's shape, the more easily to deceive and trick people. I do not like to see you go off into the mountains and wild woods with this stranger, but it would be most painful for me to deny his request. After all, he may be a very good fellow, and, as he said himself, he has come a great distance."

Godfrey was well pleased to hear these words, and thought, Grant God it is the werewolf and not a peasant from the far away mountains. I do not know yet what I am going to do, but one thing I do know: his fiendish mischief will not go unpunished.

To the herdsman he said aloud, "An old mountaineer who used to come to the valley for milk and cheese told me, too, how werewolves sometimes prowl about in human shape. But he also said they feel ill at ease in the skin of man and can easily be discovered then. For, to make themselves more comfortable, they often cast it off like an ill-suited garment, and in so doing flash a bloodshot eye or a wolf's claw. This man, however, does not act in that manner. Besides, why should he assume man's shape to lure away a little shepherd like me? Could he not, if he wished, just carry me off and do away with me, as he has done with Jackie the Homeless? He is only a common peasant, and he is hairy and ill-clad as peasants from wild mountainous regions sometimes are. It would not be right, I think, to hurt him with such suspicions and refuse his request."

"Go along with him, then, if that is your will," said the herdsman. "I will not cross you, although some uneasiness is troubling me."

Godfrey thereupon took his fiddle and, bidding farewell to the old herdsman and the boys, set forth with the stranger.

They had not gone a long way when the stranger said to Godfrey, "The sun is scorching hot today. I must take off my cap and my sheepskin."

He removed his cap and there appeared from under it not hair, but something like a wolf's pelt.

He doffed his sheepskin and his shirt which was open on his chest revealed a body covered with hair like that of a beast.

He wiped his sweaty forehead with his hand and it was as if suddenly his hand had changed to a beast's paw.

Ho, ho! thought Godfrey, but he did not say a word.

They walked on and after a while Godfrey's companion began to complain that his shoes were greatly troubling him.

144

"Take them off, sir," said Godfrey, "and you will feel more comfortable."

To which the other answered, "I would take them off gladly, only I am afraid you might be frightened when you see my feet."

"Why should I be frightened?" asked Godfrey, feigning great surprise.

"Well—because my feet are not like those you are used to."

"Why?" said Godfrey, shrugging his shoulders. "Have you hoofs on your feet, or what?"

"Well, not quite hoofs. But constant walking in the mountains has given me corns and bumps which make them look like hoofs."

"I know well how the skin sometimes toughens from walking barefoot and I am not frightened by any such thing. My grandfather had such corns on his feet that they looked like two gnarled stumps. Why shouldn't yours look like hoofs? So take them off without another thought."

The stranger was greatly pleased. "You are a clever lad," he said. And sitting down on a stone he removed his shoes. Instead of toes on his feet there were hoofs just like those of devils, only so large that Godfrey was quite astonished. Yet he showed no sign of it, but smiled and said, "Hah, you are a sissy, sir. My grandfather had larger bumps and did not groan as you do."

Thus he spoke while within him great anger welled up, and rage choked him, for he now knew for certain

K   145 what kind of farmer this was. And he would have leaped at the werewolf's throat then and there, but he remembered Jackie the Homeless, and thought: No, dear comrade, you shall not be unavenged. This cruel monster shall inflict no more harm on mankind. I will not be done away with for nothing. I will wait for a favorable moment and hold my anger in leash until I accomplish my design.

So they marched on all day and all night and at last they reached the devil's abode where the werewolf and his cronies, the witches and ogres, dwelt. It stood in the midst of steep and bare rocks, in a small and weirdly dismal glen. Godfrey was quite weary by the time they reached it, for the journey had been arduous, and the werewolf, once he had rid himself of his shoes which cumbered him greatly since he was unaccustomed to human footgear, had run so swiftly that Godfrey could hardly keep pace with him.

Therefore, when they came to the valley, Godfrey sat down on a stone and said, "You must let me rest awhile, sir."

"Rest yourself," replied the werewolf cheerfully. "Though it surprises me that it is only now you are feeling weary, because from here we can see the roofs of the houses, and the saying is that a horse runs faster once he sees the stable."

So they sat down together, and Godfrey peered about curiously, fixing in his mind every detail of this place. But, to tell the truth, there was not much to see. It

146

was a barren glen where nothing grew, and its black and hard soil suggested a big threshing floor. There was a small but deep lake almost at the far end of it, and beyond the lake there rose a hillock, huddled up against the rocks that enclosed the glen. On this very hillock the werewolf and his henchmen had put up their huts.

"What lake is that?" inquired Godfrey of the werewolf.

"That lake is called the Loch of the Drowned," returned the werewolf.

And Godfrey at once recalled what the old herdsman had told him about the lake: "The water is deep even at the short end and its mysterious whirlpools draw in the best swimmers. Nobody has ever yet come out of the lake alive."

"Well, let us go," said the werewolf, rising. "It is a pity to waste time. Indoors you will rest and refresh yourself."

They skirted the lake and started to climb up the hill where the devils' huts stood. These did not differ much from the usual peasant huts, except that they had no windows and their walls were not whitened with lime, but were blackened with tar, since evil spirits do not like white.

Each of the huts was surrounded, as is common in the country, by a little garden. But they were queer gardens, indeed. Instead of sunflowers, cats' heads grew on tall stalks and peeped intently at passers-by, blink-

They were queer gardens indeed . . .

ing their gleaming green eyes. The trees had leaves shaped like outstretched human fingers which kept curling up and straightening out, and row on row, like neatly planted cabbage-heads, grew bearded muzzles of black bucks. About the porches coiled something that looked a bit like peas and a bit like wild vine. When, however, Godfrey looked at this plant more closely he noted that its climbing stalks moved continually like a tangle of green snakes, and its flowers, shaped like long red tongues, hid and showed again, smacking greedily.

Another lad would surely have fainted with terror at such a sight, but Godfrey knew no fear. He was merely seized with loathing and great disgust but he never so much as trembled, being well aware that the werewolf was watching him intently. At last the monster stopped in front of one of the cottages and, opening the gate, entered the garden. Here he was greeted by an old dame, lean as a rod, with a thick mop of bristling hair on her head. Godfrey gazed at her, wondering what sort of freak this was, then realized that she was nothing but a plain broom prettily dressed in a skirt and bodice.

"This is the handmaid of my betrothed," said the werewolf. "She is an industrious and good girl."

And the broom began to wriggle coyly and preen herself and giggle, and veil herself with her apron, as village maidens will do.

"I am going," she said, "to give the bats a drink, because evening is falling and our cattle will wake anon."

149

Meanwhile the werewolf entered the cottage, so Godfrey followed him.

The room was completely dark, except for a fire that burned in the middle of it. In its red light Godfrey beheld a witch seated by the fire. Her face was as yellow as a lemon, her eyes gleamed like those of a cat and she had a long hooked nose and one green tooth which stuck out of her hideous mouth and reached down to her chin.

The werewolf at once presented Godfrey to her, saying he was the player who had been brought along for the next day's wedding.

"You must be very wayworn and hungry after so long a journey?" screeched the witch in a voice that resembled the squeak of ungreased wheels. "So be seated and eat, for the evening meal is ready."

And she brought forth some pots and cups which were like skulls of men and beasts and were filled with smoking food.

But Godfrey had no stomach for such devils' fare, wherefore he excused himself, saying that fatigue had got the better of his hunger. He lay down in one corner of the room and pretended to fall asleep. Yet, in real truth, he did not sleep at all, but listened closely to the conversation between the witch and the werewolf.

"Why do you take such pains with this one shepherd?" said the witch to the werewolf. "Could you not just snatch him, bring him hither and force him to play, instead of going to all the trouble of putting on the guise of man?"

"Very troublesome it was indeed," answered the werewolf and, shedding the rest of his human guise, he suddenly turned into a huge wolf with shining bloodshot eyes and horse hoofs. "Phew! I can hardly breathe. Still, I could not do otherwise, for had I snatched the boy and dragged him hither, forcing him to play, he would scarcely be alive from fright and his music would not be very gay to dance to. Now, this is to be a wedding the like of which has not yet been witnessed. It isn't every day that a werewolf weds a witch."

Ho, ho, I will treat you to some wedding, thought Godfrey, still pretending to be asleep, and even snoring occasionally.

"You are right," agreed the witch. "You have contrived this wisely. But tell me, what do you propose to do with him afterward?"

The werewolf broke into laughter, exhibiting his sharp white fangs, and retorted with a grin, "Me-thinks a roast of the fiddler would be no worse than any other. We will eat him together with that other herdboy whom I carried away from their valley last week."

"I have been trying to fatten him up but he is still as skinny as a lath," said the witch wryly.

At these words Godfrey was overjoyed, and thought: So you are still alive, Jackie dear. Well, please God, I will set you free, and together we shall return safe and sound to the valley.

For he had already formed his scheme to destroy the ogres, witches and the werewolf and deliver the whole region of the devil-sent plague. So he kept listening to what the witch was whispering to the werewolf.

"We are talking too loud," she said. "The boy might hear us."

"Don't be silly," replied the werewolf. "See, he is fast asleep."

And he laughed again.

"He is not so clever. He has not the slightest notion of where he is. He is a frightfully stupid boy."

Godfrey listened no longer. Now that he knew all he want to learn, he resolved to rest awhile. He fell asleep and slept soundly not only through that night, but through nearly all the next day as well, so weary was he from the exertion of the journey.

He was at length aroused by the preparations which the witch and the werewolf, aided by the broom, were making for the wedding.

"We shall have to clear the room," said the witch, "because once the dancing gets under way we will need every bit of space."

"That will not help much," sighed the werewolf. "The room is so small and the guests will be many."

"I know a way to avoid a crush," remarked Godfrey unexpectedly, for he had been listening closely to the conversation.

"Now, what would you suggest?" queried the werewolf.

"If you want my advice," said Godfrey, "then do not dance indoors, but down in the valley by the lake. It is going to be a moonlit night, there will be plenty of room for dancing, and since there are no bushes or stones and the ground is level and hard, you will be more comfortable than inside. You can dance in the valley on one side of the lake while I stand on the other, on the hill, and play for you. Because of the mountains all around, the music will be echoed loud and clear throughout the valley."

"By my dear devil!" exclaimed the werewolf, who had forgotten that he was supposed to be a peasant. "By my dear devil, the lad is right."

The witch, however, was possessed of more sagacity than the werewolf, a woman being commonly shrewder than a man. So she said to Godfrey, "That is good advice about the valley. But tell me, why is it you want to stand on the other side of the lake when you play right amongst us in the valley?"

"I will explain," replied Godfrey. "You must have heard how, when I strike up a lively tune in my sweeping manner, nobody and nothing can stand still, but all must instantly start to dance and keep at it for as long as their breath holds. Well, if I should be standing in your midst, you would jostle me ever and again and hinder me from playing. And then, too, I would fain watch your dancing, and it will be much easier for me to see you from the hill than if I should stand in the middle of the crush, in the throng."

"Have it your way, then," acquiesced the witch, having dismissed her suspicions.

And straightway she ran off to invite the guests to the valley.

Ugh, 'twas a sight and something to wonder at when the guests began to assemble!

Horrible witches there were galore, those who will harm men in no time, and ogres and bogies which feed on human blood, and goblins who lead travelers astray on foggy nights. In the bright moonlight Godfrey could see clearly from his hill as the gathering paired off for dancing. They were overjoyed at having such a fiddler to play for them, for usually at devils' weddings the only music is the whistling of the wind and the croaking of toads.

Well, thought Godfrey, with God's help this shall be your last dance. And he drew the bow across the strings.

Ho! So sprightly and rousing was the music which resounded through the valley that not only the ogres, witches and goblins, led by the werewolf, began to dance; but even the brooms, who, as is well known, are in attendance upon witches, ran out of the huts and started whirling with their mistresses.

And the dancing grew ever more frenzied, ever giddier, until the dancers' breath failed, sparks began to fly before their eyes, and reason left their heads.

The witches thrust their claws into one another, and danced on.

The ogres and goblins took each other by the hand and spun about, howling and whistling with glee so loud that the wind scurried all over the valley and the bats, startled by the wild uproar, fled in swarms from the devils' huts.

The brooms lost their skirts and bodices and thrashed about right and left with such fury that from sheer impetus one and then another slashed her mistress on the pate.

In the middle was the werewolf himself, dancing, stamping his hoofs, flashing his bloodshot eyes and showing his sharp fangs.

Ha, you will not rejoice long, son of the devil, thought Godfrey, and struck the strings even more violently.

And the whole fiendish lot surged forward in one solid mass, lured onward by the irresistible call of the dance music and unmindful of the bottomless lake that separated them from the fiddler.

Perhaps one or another would have come to his senses and stopped, but the dance-drunk crowd swept him forward and carried him along.

And the fiddle kept calling from the other shore of the lake, ever louder, ever more insistently.

Onward, onward, this way, this way, the music seemed to say.

Just at the water's edge, the crowd seemed to waver, but drunk with the music and completely senseless, it plunged straight into the lake.

Thus it was that Godfrey freed the whole region of

the werewolf, the ogres, witches and goblins—the whole
devilish crew. In one of the huts he found Jackie the
Homeless and other shepherds whom the werewolf
had kept imprisoned, all of whom his music had saved
from horrible death.

Great joy reigned in all the valleys and throughout
the region, and the fame of Godfrey's songs, which had
such power that even the devils could not resist them,
spread not only over the mountains but through the
length and breadth of the land until it reached the
royal court.

Cobbler, Cobbler,
Mend My Shoe

By JAN STRUTHER

There are a great many strange characters wandering about the streets of that strange little town they call Chelsea. There are street singers by the score, and street musicians who play on barrel organs and hurdy-gurdies and cornets and flutes and fiddles and harps. There are men who shout "Fine Log—O!" and men who want your chairs, and women who cry "Wonchu buy my sweet bloomin' lavender, sixteen fine bunshes for one penny"—which sounds very poetic but is actually a lie, because prices have risen since the day when the cry was first invented. There are also several religious maniacs, old men with grey beards and young men with golden ones, who walk about bareheaded and talk of God. Finally, there are a few artists in broad floppy felt hats and black cloaks, and a great many female cranks who think that they can bring about the renaissance of Art by wearing laboriously hand-woven clothes of pastel colouring and quite intolerable cut. In fact,

This story is from A Pocketful of Pebbles *by Jan Struther*

there are so many queer-looking people of one kind and
another that after a while you don't bother to turn
round and stare at them as you did when you first came
to live there.

Nobody stared, therefore, at the old man who walked
up the High Street one afternoon in late October, when
the chilly autumn sunset was just beginning to send people home to hot buttered toast and the passionate rap-
ture of first fires. He was a very old man indeed, and
a very odd old man. From the long loose cloak that he
wore he might have been one of the artists, but from
the raggedness of it you would have classed him with
the hurdy-gurdists. The white beard and a touch of
far-away ecstasy in the eyes seemed to label him "religious"; while his sandalled feet were faintly suggestive
of the cranky and hand-woven women.

Not sandalled feet—sandalled foot. For his left foot
was bare and very dirty, and his left sandal he was carrying in his gnarled old hand, because one of the straps
of it was broken. And as he walked along, limping a
little from a cut on his foot, he muttered, "Who is going to mend my sandal?"

Presently he came to a shop whose windows were
decked with innumerable shoes, as the firmament is
decked with stars. There were men's shoes marked
"Highly serviceable," and women's shoes marked
"Very chic," and felt bedroom slippers marked "Un-
rivalled bargain." The old man stopped and gazed into
the window.

"Hideous—most hideous," he murmured, and mused upon the decadence of the times. Then he caught sight of some children's sandals in a corner, and the sternness of his face relaxed.

"But the children still wear sandals," he said, softly; and reassured by this he went into the shop. Inside there was a bright and ugly green carpet, and his bare foot left a trail of mud and blood upon it as he walked. A young salesman appeared from the depths of the shop rubbing his hands and saying mechanically, "Good afternoon, sir. What can I do for you?" But when he had looked more closely at the old man in the failing light his tone changed.

"Excuse me, sir—the carpet. Something's wrong with your foot."

"I know," said the old man patiently; "I have damaged it on some broken vessel. That is why I came in here. I want you to mend my sandal so that I may wear it again." He held out the tattered footgear to the young man, who peered at it distastefully with his hands behind his back.

"I'm afraid you'll have to go somewhere else," he said, dropping the "sir." "We don't do repairs."

"Will you sell me another pair, then?"

"We don't stock anything like that, I'm afraid."

"But those ones in the window—?"

"Oh, for children, yes. No demand for large sizes."

"As ever," murmured the old man, "the children are the wise ones. Can you not make me some, then?"

"Sorry," said the salesman, shortly, "but we're not manufacturers, we're only agents. Good afternoon." Very firmly, he held the door open, and very sadly the old man passed out muttering to himself, "You cannot make, neither can you mend, are there no craftsmen left?"

There were three more shops of the same kind in the High Street, and at each of the three he met with the same treatment. In one of them the salesman called the manager, and the manager requested him to leave. In another a pert young woman told him with a giggle that they hadn't got any hare skins or rabbit skins to-day, thank you. In the third he was so tired that he sat down, uninvited, on one of the red plush chairs, but the manager fixed him with a glassy eye and began to talk about the police, so he rose wearily to his feet again and shuffled away down the street.

"In all this great city," he asked himself, "will nobody mend my shoes?"

But suddenly there were quick running footsteps behind him, and a girl in a black frock touched his arm. She was a little button-nosed creature, a very unimportant assistant in the last shop he had entered, and she had felt sorry for the old man.

"Look here," she panted, "my uncle's a cobbler in Emily Street. You try 'im." And she scuttled back to the shop, blushing at her own impulsiveness. The old man turned and threw a blessing after her as she ran. (And it is a certain fact that the very next day the manager told her she was getting on much better now, and her friend Mabel gave her an almost-new blue hat because she herself had gone into mourning, and she picked up a shilling in the gutter going home, and the boy she was walking out with asked her to marry him. So you may say what you like about blessings.)

The old man limped along to Emily Street, which is a little alley leading off the High Street. And there, sure enough, was a real old-fashioned cobbler's shop, with a battered wooden counter that was also a workbench, and bundles of boot laces hanging like seaweed on the walls, and little irregular three-cornered scraps of hide littering the floor, and a glorious, all-pervading smell of leather. And there at the bench, bent double over his work under a flaming, fan-shaped gas-jet, was Mr. Mullins, the cobbler. He looked up with a cheerful grin as the old man entered. He liked queer-looking customers.

"I wonder," said the old man diffidently, "whether you can mend my shoe?"

"Mend your shoe, sir? If it's anything made of leather, I can mend it. That's my trade, that is."

"At last," cried the old man, handing him the sandal, "I have found a craftsman!"

"That's a curious shoe," said Mullins, looking at it with interest. "If you'll excuse my saying so, I bet that's carried you a good long way in its time?"

"Sixteen hundred years," the old man murmured.

"Potty," thought Mullins to himself, "but a decent

old cove." Aloud he said, "I'll do this 'ere job for you now if you like, seeing you won't want to walk 'ome as you are. If you'd care to take a seat . . ." He pushed forward a high wooden stool. "Live far from 'ere?"

"A good long way," answered the old man, and he leaned forward, watching with keen interest in his face while the other worked.

"If you don't mind my saying so, sir, this is the finest bit of leather ever I see. Even if it is old."

"Yes. Leather was leather in those days."

"I don't know when I've seen such a beautiful bit of leather," Mullins repeated. "If you'll excuse me, sir, may I ask where you got this pair of sandals?"

"I made them myself. You see, I was in your trade once."

"Was you now? Well, I never. Well, well. All I can say is, you knew your job. Give it up now, 'ave you?"

"Yes. A long time ago."

"Ar. Sold the good-will, I suppose?"

"Good-will—ah, that's neither bought nor sold," said the old man.

" 'Tis in London," Mullins assured him. "But per'aps other places they've got other ways of doing business. Now where was it you was working exactly?"

"In Soissons," said the old man.

"Soissong? Not Soissong on the Aisne?"

"You know the place?" asked the old man, eagerly.

"I should think I ought to. I was there two years— there and thereabouts—before I was knocked out."

"A beautiful place," the old man mused, "but a hot-bed of evil-doing and evil-thinking. A veritable hot-bed."

"A bloody 'otbed," agreed Mullins, tersely. " 'ottest corner I was ever in, anyway."

"I did my best, you know, I did my best. . . . Living among them and working among them, and trying to reach their immortal souls through the soles of their shoes. They were hard to convert, but perhaps . . ."

His voice trailed away, and for a few minutes the two men lost themselves among the memories of old fights; only for one of them it was the fighting of armies, and for the other it was the fighting of God against the gods. And one of them had travelled back scarcely a decade, while the other was dwelling on things that had happened sixteen hundred years ago.

"There now," said Mr. Mullins, putting the finishing touches to the sandal. "I think you'll find that all right. Don't you move, sir. I'll just slip it on for you."

He knelt down among the scraps of leather and fastened the sandal on to the bare and travel-stained foot. And then the extraordinary old man laid his wrinkled hand on Mullins's head and began to bless him.

Mullins thought, "Lumme, this is a go." The old cove must be one of the religious ones after all, who come and ask you whether you're saved. He was glad there was nobody there to see him being made a fool of. And then suddenly he came all over queer, and felt happier than

163

he ever had before, and rather lightheaded. He couldn't see properly. His head swam . . .

It was only for a moment, but when he came to himself again the old man had gone away, and on the counter lay a gold coin. It wasn't a sovereign—it was a foreign coin, and it looked very old and worn. He slipped it into his pocket hastily because his small son Tommy had suddenly burst into the shop, swinging his school satchel.

"Oh, Dad! Do you know what we done 'safternoon? A play! At least, a bit of a play. Shakespeare. And we read it out in turns. And, Dad—I was the King, I was!"

"Whatever are you talking about?" asked Mullins, patiently. "What King? What play?"

"Henry the Fifth. Look here—you read it yourself." He pushed a paper-covered Shakespeare under his father's nose.

"Oh—poetry!" Mullins sniffed.

"Go on, Dad. It's lovely. Just read the end bit of what the King says—"

. . . And gentlemen in England now a-bed
Shall think themselves accursed they were not here,
And hold their manhoods cheap whiles any speaks
That fought with us upon Saint Crispin's day.

"You see, today is S'n Crispin's day—twenty-fiff of October. That's why Teacher made us do it today."

"Oh," said Mullins, unimpressed. "All this play-acting stuff. Why can't they teach you something useful? And 'oo is Saint Crispin, any'ow, when 'e's at 'ome?"

"'e was a shoemaker—just like you are," cried Tommy triumphantly. "An' Teacher said 'e wos the pattern—pattron—patron saint of shoemakers—so there!"

"Wos 'e now?" said Mullins, slowly, scratching his head. Then after a long pause—

"Oh, 'e wos, wos 'e?" said Mullins, thoughtfully, fingering the gold coin in his pocket.

The Devil and Daniel Webster

By STEPHEN VINCENT BENET

I

It's a story they tell in the border country, where Massachusetts joins Vermont and New Hampshire.

Yes, Dan'l Webster's dead—or, at least, they buried him. But every time there's a thunderstorm around Marshfield, they say you can hear his rolling voice in the hollows of the sky. And they say that if you go to his grave and speak loud and clear, "Dan'l Webster— Dan'l Webster!" the ground'll begin to shiver and the trees begin to shake. And after a while you'll hear a deep voice saying, "Neighbor, how stands the Union?" Then you better answer the Union stands as she stood, rock-bottomed and copper-sheathed, one and indivisible, or he's liable to rear right out of the ground. At least, that's what I was told when I was a youngster.

You see, for a while, he was the biggest man in the country. He never got to be President, but he was the biggest man. There were thousands that trusted in him

This story is from Selected Works of Stephen Vincent Benet *by Stephen Vincent Benet*

166

right next to God Almighty, and they told stories about him and all the things that belonged to him that were like the stories of patriarchs and such. They said, when he stood up to speak, stars and stripes came right out in the sky, and once he spoke against a river and made it sink into the ground. They said, when he walked the woods with his fishing rod, Killall, the trout would jump out of the streams right into his pockets, for they knew it was no use putting up a fight against him; and, when he argued a case, he could turn on the harps of the blessed and the shaking of the earth underground. That was the kind of man he was, and his big farm up at Marshfield was suitable to him. The chickens he raised were all white meat down through the drumsticks, the cows were tended like children, and the big ram he called Goliath had horns with a curl like a morning-glory vine and could butt through an iron door. But Dan'l wasn't one of your gentlemen farmers; he knew all the ways of the land, and he'd be up by candlelight to see that the chores got done. A man with a mouth like a mastiff, a brow like a mountain and eyes like burning anthracite—that was Dan'l Webster in his prime. And the biggest case he argued never got written down in the books, for he argued it against the devil, nip and tuck and no holds barred. And this is the way I used to hear it told.

There was a man named Jabez Stone, lived at Cross Corners, New Hampshire. He wasn't a bad man to start with, but he was an unlucky man. If he planted corn, he got borers; if he planted potatoes, he got blight. He had good-enough land, but it didn't prosper him; he had a decent wife and children, but the more children he had, the less there was to feed them. If stones cropped up in his neighbor's field, boulders boiled up in his; if he had a horse with the spavins, he'd trade it for one with the staggers and give something extra. There's some folks bound to be like that, apparently. But one day Jabez got sick of the whole business.

He'd been plowing that morning and he'd just broke the plowshare on a rock that he could have sworn hadn't been there yesterday. And, as he stood looking at the plowshare, the off horse began to cough—that ropy kind of cough that means sickness and horse doctors. There were two children down with the measles, his wife was ailing, and he had a whitlow on his thumb. It was about the last straw for Jabez Stone. "I vow," he said, and he looked around him kind of desperate— "I vow it's enough to make a man want to sell his soul to the devil! And I would, too, for two cents!"

Then he felt a kind of queerness come over him at having said what he'd said; though, naturally, being a New Hampshireman, he wouldn't take it back. But all the same, when it got to be evening, and as far as he could see, no notice had been taken, he felt relieved in his mind, for he was a religious man. But notice is always taken, sooner or later, just like the Good Book says. And, sure enough, next day, about supper-time, a soft-spoken, dark-dressed stranger drove up in a handsome buggy and asked for Jabez Stone.

Well, Jabez told his family it was a lawyer, come to see him about a legacy. But he knew who it was. He didn't like the looks of the stranger, nor the way he smiled with his teeth. They were white teeth, and plentiful—some say they were filed to a point, but I wouldn't vouch for that. And he didn't like it when the dog took one look at the stranger and ran away howling, with his tail between his legs. But having passed his word, more or less, he stuck to it, and they went out behind the barn and made their bargain. Jabez Stone had to prick his finger to sign, and the stranger lent him a silver pen. The wound healed clean, but it left a little white scar.

II

After that, all of a sudden, things began to pick up and prosper for Jabez Stone. His cows got fat, and his horses sleek, his crops were the envy of the neighborhood, and lightning might strike all over the valley, but it wouldn't strike his barn. Pretty soon, he was one of the prosperous people of the county; they asked him to run for selectman, and he stood for it; there began to be talk of running him for state senate. All in all, you might say the Stone family was as happy and contented as cats in a dairy. And so they were, except for Jabez Stone.

He'd been contented enough, the first few years. It's a great thing when bad luck turns; it drives most other things out of your head. True, every now and then, especially in rainy weather, the little white scar on his finger would give him a twinge. And once a year, punctual as clockwork, the stranger with the handsome buggy would come driving by. But the sixth year, the stranger lighted, and, after that, his peace was over for Jabez Stone.

The stranger came up through the lower field, switching his boots with a cane—they were handsome black boots, but Jabez Stone never liked the look of them, particularly the toes. And, after he'd passed the time of day, he said, "Well, Mr. Stone, you're a hummer! It's a very pretty property you've got here, Mr. Stone."

"Well, some might favor it and others might not," said Jabez Stone, for he was a New Hampshireman.

"Oh, no need to decry your industry!" said the stranger, very easy, showing his teeth in a smile. "After all, we know what's been done, and it's been according to contract and specifications. So when—ahem—the mortgage falls due next year, you shouldn't have any regrets."

"Speaking of that mortgage, mister," said Jabez Stone, and he looked around for help to the earth and the sky, "I'm beginning to have one or two doubts about it."

"Doubts?" said the stranger, not quite so pleasantly.

"Why, yes," said Jabez Stone. "This being the U.S.A. and me always having been a religious man." He cleared his throat and got bolder. "Yes, sir," he said, "I'm beginning to have considerable doubts as to that mortgage holding in court."

"There's courts and courts," said the stranger, clicking his teeth. "Still, we might as well have a look at the original document." And he hauled out a big black pocketbook, full of papers. "Sherwin, Slater, Stevens, Stone," he muttered. "I, Jabez Stone, for a term of seven years—Oh, it's quite in order, I think."

But Jabez Stone wasn't listening, for he saw something else flutter out of the black pocketbook. It was something that looked like a moth, but it wasn't a moth. And as Jabez Stone stared at it, it seemed to speak to him in a small sort of piping voice, terribly small and thin, but terribly human.

"Neighbor Stone!" it squeaked. "Neighbor Stone! Help me! For God's sake, help me!"

But before Jabez could stir hand or foot, the stranger whipped out a big bandanna handkerchief, caught the creature in it, just like a butterfly, and started tying up the ends of the bandanna.

"Sorry for the interruption," he said. "As I was saying—"

But Jabez Stone was shaking all over like a scared horse.

"That's Miser Stevens' voice!" he said, in a croak. "And you've got him in your handkerchief!"

171

The stranger looked a little embarrassed.

"Yes, I really should have transferred him to the collecting box," he said with a simper, "but there were some rather unusual specimens there and I didn't want them crowded. Well, well, these little contretemps will occur."

"I don't know what you mean by contertan," said Jabez Stone, "but that was Miser Stevens' voice! And he ain't dead! You can't tell me he is! He was just as spry and mean as a woodchuck, Tuesday!"

"In the midst of life—" said the stranger, kind of pious. "Listen!" Then a bell began to toll in the valley and Jabez Stone listened, with the sweat running down his face. For he knew it was tolling for Miser Stevens and that he was dead.

"These long-standing accounts," said the stranger with a sigh; "one really hates to close them. But business is business."

He still had the bandanna in his hand, and Jabez felt sick as he saw the cloth struggle and flutter.

"Are they all as small as that?" he asked hoarsely.

"Small?" said the stranger. "Oh, I see what you mean. Why, they vary." He measured Jabez Stone with his eyes, and his teeth showed. "Don't worry, Mr. Stone," he said. "You'll go with a very good grade. I wouldn't trust you outside the collecting box. Now, a man like Dan'l Webster, of course—well, we'd have to build a special box for him, and even at that, I imagine the wing spread would astonish you. He'd certainly be a prize. I wish we could see our way clear to him. But, in your case, as I was saying—"

"Put that handkerchief away!" said Jabez Stone, and he began to beg and to pray. But the best he could get at the end was a three years' extension, with conditions.

But till you make a bargain like that, you've got no idea how fast four years can run. By the last months of those years, Jabez Stone's known all over the state and there's talk of running him for governor—and it's dust and ashes in his mouth. For every day, when he gets up, he thinks, "There's one more night gone," and every night when he lies down, he thinks of the black pocketbook and the soul of Miser Stevens, and it makes him sick at heart. Till, finally, he can't bear it any longer, and, in the last days of the last year, he hitches up his horse and drives off to seek Dan'l Webster. For Dan'l was born in New Hampshire, only a few miles from Cross Corners, and it's well known that he has a particular soft spot for old neighbors.

III

It was early in the morning when he got to Marshfield, but Dan'l was up already talking Latin to the farm hands and wrestling with the ram, Goliath, and trying out a new trotter and working up speeches to make against John C. Calhoun. But when he heard a New Hampshireman had come to see him, he dropped everything else he was doing, for that was Dan'l's way. He gave Jabez Stone a breakfast that five men couldn't eat, went into the living history of every man and woman in Cross Corners, and finally asked him how he could serve him.

Jabez Stone allowed that it was a kind of mortgage case. "Well, I haven't pleaded a mortgage case in a long time, and I don't generally plead now, except before the Supreme Court," said Dan'l, "but if I can, I'll help you."

"Then I've got hope for the first time in ten years," said Jabez Stone, and told him the details.

Dan'l walked up and down as he listened, hands behind his back, now and then asking a question, now and then plunging his eyes at the floor, as if they'd bore through it like gimlets. When Jabez had finished, Dan'l puffed out his cheeks and blew. Then he turned to Jabez Stone and a smile broke over his face like the sunrise over Monadnock.

"You've certainly given yourself the devil's own row to hoe, Neighbor Stone," he said, "but I'll take your case."

"You'll take it?" said Jabez Stone, hardly daring to believe.

"Yes," said Dan'l Webster. "I've got about seventy-five other things to do and the Missouri Compromise to straighten out, but I'll take your case. For if two New Hampshiremen aren't a match for the devil, we might as well give the country back to the Indians."

Then he shook Jabez Stone by the hand and said, "Did you come down here in a hurry?"

"Well, I admit I made time," said Jabez Stone.

"You'll go back faster," said Dan'l Webster, and he told 'em to hitch up Constitution and Constellation to the carriage. They were matched grays with one white forefoot, and they stepped like greased lightning.

Well, I won't describe how excited and pleased the whole Stone family was to have the great Dan'l Webster for a guest, when they finally got there. Jabez Stone had lost his hat on the way, blown off when they overtook the wind, but he didn't take much account of that. But after supper he sent the family off to bed, for he had most particular business with Mr. Webster. Mrs. Stone wanted them to sit in the front parlor, but Dan'l Webster knew front parlors and said he preferred the kitchen. So it was there they sat, waiting for the stranger, with a jug on the table between them and a bright fire on the hearth—the stranger being scheduled to show up on the stroke of midnight, according to specifications.

Well, most men wouldn't have asked for better company than Dan'l Webster and a jug. But with every tick of the clock Jabez Stone got sadder and sadder. His eyes roved round, and though he sampled the jug you could see he couldn't taste it. Finally, on the stroke of 11:30 he reached over and grabbed Dan'l Webster by the arm.

"Mr. Webster, Mr. Webster!" he said, and his voice

175

was shaking with fear and a desperate courage. "For God's sake, Mr. Webster, harness your horses and get away from this place while you can!"

"You've brought me a long way, neighbor, to tell me you don't like my company," said Dan'l Webster, quite peaceable, pulling at the jug.

"Miserable wretch that I am!" groaned Jabez Stone. "I've brought you a devilish way, and now I see my folly. Let him take me if he wills. I don't hanker after it, I must say, but I can stand it. But you're the Union's stay and New Hampshire's pride! He mustn't get you, Mr. Webster! He mustn't get you!"

Dan'l Webster looked at the distracted man, all gray and shaking in the firelight, and laid a hand on his shoulder.

"I'm obliged to you, Neighbor Stone," he said gently. "It's kindly thought of. But there's a jug on the table and a case in hand. And I never left a jug or a case half finished in my life."

And just at that moment there was a sharp rap on the door.

"Ah," said Dan'l Webster, very coolly, "I thought your clock was a trifle slow, Neighbor Stone." He stepped to the door and opened it. "Come in!" he said.

The stranger came in—very dark and tall he looked in the firelight. He was carrying a box under his arm —a black, japanned box with little air holes in the lid. At the sight of the box, Jabez Stone gave a low cry and shrank into a corner of the room.

"Mr. Webster, I presume," said the stranger, very polite, but with his eyes glowing like a fox's deep in the woods.

"Attorney of record for Jabez Stone," said Dan'l Webster, but his eyes were glowing too. "Might I ask your name?"

"I've gone by a good many," said the stranger carelessly. "Perhaps Scratch will do for the evening. I'm often called that in these regions."

Then he sat down at the table and poured himself a drink from the jug. The liquor was cold in the jug, but it came steaming into the glass.

"And now," said the stranger, smiling and showing his teeth, "I shall call upon you, as a law-abiding citizen, to assist me in taking possession of my property."

Well, with that the argument began—and it went hot and heavy. At first, Jabez Stone had a flicker of hope, but when he saw Dan'l Webster being forced back at point after point, he just sat scrunched in his corner, with his eyes on that japanned box. For there wasn't any doubt as to the deed or the signature—that was the worst of it. Dan'l Webster twisted and turned and thumped his fist on the table, but he couldn't get away from that. He offered to compromise the case; the stranger wouldn't hear of it. He pointed out the property had increased in value, and state senators ought to be worth more; the stranger stuck to the letter of the law. He was a great lawyer, Dan'l Webster, but we know who's the King of Lawyers, as the Good Book tells us, and it seemed as if, for the first time, Dan'l Webster had met his match.

Finally, the stranger yawned a little. "Your spirited efforts on behalf of your client do you credit, Mr. Webster," he said, "but if you have no more arguments to adduce, I'm rather pressed for time—" and Jabez Stone shuddered.

Dan'l Webster's brow looked dark as a thundercloud. "Pressed or not, you shall not have this man!" he thundered. "Mr. Stone is an American citizen, and no American citizen may be forced into the service of a foreign prince. We fought England for that in '12 and we'll fight all hell for it again!"

"Foreign?" said the stranger. "And who calls me a foreigner?"

"Well, I never yet heard of the dev—of your claiming American citizenship," said Dan'l Webster in surprise.

"And who with better right?" said the stranger, with one of his terrible smiles. "When the first wrong was done to the first Indian, I was there. When the first slaver put out for the Congo, I stood on her deck. Am I not in your books and stories and beliefs, from the first settlements on? Am I not spoken of, still, in every church in New England? 'Tis true the North claims me for a Southerner, and the South for a Northerner, but I am neither. I am merely an honest American like yourself—and of the best descent—for, to tell the truth,

Mr. Webster, though I don't like to boast of it, my name is older in this country than yours."

"Aha!" said Dan'l Webster, with the veins standing out in his forehead. "Then I stand on the Constitution! I demand a trial for my client!"

"The case is hardly one for an ordinary court," said the stranger, his eyes flickering. "And, indeed, the lateness of the hour—"

"Let it be any court you choose, so it is an American judge and an American jury!" said Dan'l Webster in his pride. "Let it be the quick or the dead; I'll abide the issue!"

"You have said it," said the stranger, and pointed his finger at the door. And with that, and all of a sudden, there was a rushing of wind outside and a noise of footsteps. They came, clear and distinct, through the night. And yet, they were not like the footsteps of living men.

"In God's name, who comes by so late?" cried Jabez Stone, in an ague of fear.

"The jury Mr. Webster demands," said the stranger, sipping at his boiling glass. "You must pardon the rough appearance of one or two; they will have come a long way."

IV

And with that the fire burned blue and the door blew open and twelve men entered, one by one.

If Jabez Stone had been sick with terror before, he

was blind with terror now. For there was Walter Butler, the loyalist, who spread fire and horror through
the Mohawk Valley in the times of the Revolution; and
there was Simon Girty, the renegade, who saw white
men burned at the stake and whooped with the Indians
to see them burn. His eyes were green, like a cata-
mount's, and the stains on his hunting shirt did not
come from the blood of a deer. King Philip was there,
wild and proud as he had been in life, with the great
gash in his head that gave him his death wound, and
cruel Governor Dale, who broke men on the wheel.
There was Morton of Merry Mount, who so vexed the
Plymouth Colony, with his flushed, loose, handsome
face and his hate of the godly. There was Teach, the
bloody pirate, with his black beard curling on his
breast. The Reverend John Smeet, with his strangler's
hands and his Geneva gown, walked as daintily as he
had to the gallows. The red print of the rope was still
around his neck, but he carried a perfumed handkerchief in one hand. One and all, they came into the room
with the fires of hell still upon them, and the stranger
named their names and their deed as they came, till the
tale of twelve was told. Yet the stranger had told the
truth—they had all played a part in America.

"Are you satisfied with the jury, Mr. Webster?" said
the stranger mockingly, when they had taken their
places.

The sweat stood upon Dan'l Webster's brow, but his
voice was clear.

"Quite satisfied," he said. "Though I miss General Arnold from the company."

"Benedict Arnold is engaged upon other business," said the stranger, with a glower. "Ah, you asked for a justice, I believe."

He pointed his finger once more, and a tall man, soberly clad in Puritan garb, with the burning gaze of the fanatic, stalked into the room and took his judge's place.

"Justice Hathorne is a jurist of experience," said the stranger. "He presided at certain witch trials once held in Salem. There were others who repented of the business later, but not he."

"Repent of such notable wonders and undertakings?" said the stern old justice. "Nay, hang them—hang them all!" And he muttered to himself in a way that struck ice into the soul of Jabez Stone.

Then the trial began, and, as you might expect, it didn't look anyways good for the defense. And Jabez Stone didn't make much of a witness in his own behalf. He took one look at Simon Girty and screeched, and they had to put him back in his corner in a kind of swoon.

It didn't halt the trial, though; the trial went on, as trials do. Dan'l Webster had faced some hard juries and hanging judges in his time, but this was the hardest he'd ever faced, and he knew it. They sat there with a kind of glitter in their eyes, and the stranger's smooth voice went on and on. Every time he'd raise an objection, it'd be "Objection sustained," but whenever Dan'l objected, it'd be "Objection denied." Well, you couldn't expect fair play from a fellow like this Mr. Scratch.

It got to Dan'l in the end, and he began to heat, like iron in the forge. When he got up to speak he was going to flay that stranger with every trick known to the law, and the judge and jury too. He didn't care if it was contempt of court or what would happen to him for it. He didn't care any more what happened to Jabez Stone. He just got madder and madder, thinking of what he'd say. And yet, curiously enough, the more he thought about it, the less he was able to arrange his speech in his mind.

Till, finally, it was time for him to get up on his feet, and he did so, all ready to bust out with lightnings and denunciations. But before he started he looked over the judge and jury for a moment, such being his custom. And he noticed the glitter in their eyes was twice as strong as before, and they all leaned forward. Like hounds just before they get the fox, they looked, and the blue mist of evil in the room thickened as he watched them. Then he saw what he'd been about to do, and he wiped his forehead, as a man might who's just escaped falling into a pit in the dark.

For it was him they'd come for, not only Jabez Stone. He read it in the glitter of their eyes and in the way the stranger hid his mouth with one hand. And if he fought them with their own weapons, he'd fall into their power; he knew that, though he couldn't have told you how. It was his own anger and horror that burned in their eyes; and he'd have to wipe that out or the case was lost. He stood there for a moment, his black eyes burning like anthracite. And then he began to speak.

He started off in a low voice, though you could hear every word. They say he could call on the harps of the blessed when he chose. And this was just as simple and easy as a man could talk. But he didn't start out by condemning or reviling. He was talking about the things that make a country a country, and a man a man.

And he began with the simple things that everybody's known and felt—the freshness of a fine morning when you're young, and the taste of food when you're hungry, and the new day that's every day when you're a child. He took them up and he turned them in his hands. They were good things for any man. But without freedom, they sickened. And when he talked of those enslaved, and the sorrows of slavery, his voice got like a big bell. It wasn't a spread-eagle speech, but he made you see it. He admitted all the wrong that had ever been done. But he showed how, out of the wrong and the right, the suffering and the starvations, something new had come. And everybody had played a part in it, even the traitors.

Then he turned to Jabez Stone and showed him as he was—an ordinary man who'd had hard luck and wanted to change it. And, because he'd wanted to change it, now he was going to be punished for all eter-

nity. And yet there was good in Jabez Stone, and he
showed that good. He was hard and mean, in some
ways, but he was a man. There was sadness in being a
man, but it was a proud thing too. And he showed what
the pride of it was till you couldn't help feeling it. Yes,
even in hell, if a man was a man, you'd know it. And he
wasn't pleading for any one person any more, though
his voice rang like an organ. He was telling the story
and the failures and the endless journey of mankind.
They got tricked and trapped and bamboozled, but it
was a great journey. And no demon that was ever foaled
could know the inwardness of it—it took a man to do
that.

V

The fire began to die on the hearth and the wind before morning to blow. The light was getting gray in
the room when Dan'l Webster finished. And his words
came back at the end to New Hampshire ground, and
the one spot of land that each man loves and clings to.
He painted a picture of that, and to each one of that
jury he spoke of things long forgotten. For his voice
could search the heart, and that was his gift and
strength. And to one, his voice was like the forest and
its secrecy, and to another like the sea and the storms
of the sea; and one heard the cry of his lost nation in
it, and another saw a little harmless scene he hadn't remembered for years. But each saw something. And

when Dan'l Webster finished he didn't know whether or not he'd saved Jabez Stone. But he knew he'd done a miracle. For the glitter was gone from the eyes of judge and jury, and, for the moment, they were men again, and knew they were men.

"The defense rests," said Dan'l Webster, and stood there like a mountain. His ears were still ringing with his speech, and he didn't hear anything else till he heard Judge Hathorne say, "The jury will retire to consider its verdict."

Walter Butler rose in his place and his face had a dark, gay pride on it.

"The jury has considered its verdict," he said, and looked the stranger full in the eye. "We find for the defendant, Jabez Stone."

With that, the smile left the stranger's face, but Walter Butler did not flinch.

"Perhaps 'tis not strictly in accordance with the evidence," he said, "but even the damned may salute the eloquence of Mr. Webster."

With that, the long crow of a rooster split the gray morning sky, and judge and jury were gone from the room like a puff of smoke and as if they had never been there. The stranger turned to Dan'l Webster, smiling wryly. "Major Butler was always a bold man," he said. "I had not thought him quite so bold. Nevertheless, my congratulations, as between two gentlemen."

"I'll have that paper first, if you please," said Dan'l Webster, and he took it and tore it into four pieces. It was queerly warm to the touch. "And now," he said, "I'll have you!" and his hand came down like a bear trap on the stranger's arm. For he knew that once you had bested anybody like Mr. Scratch in fair fight, his power on you was gone. And he could see that Mr. Scratch knew it too.

The stranger twisted and wriggled, but he couldn't get out of that grip. "Come, come, Mr. Webster," he said, smiling palely. "This sort of thing is ridic—ouch! —is ridiculous. If you're worried about the costs of the case, naturally, I'd be glad to pay—"

"And so you shall!" said Dan'l Webster, shaking him till his teeth rattled. "For you'll sit right down at that table and draw up a document, promising never to bother Jabez Stone nor his heirs or assigns nor any other New Hampshireman till doomsday! For any hades we want to raise in this state, we can raise ourselves, without assistance from strangers."

"Ouch!" said the stranger. "Ouch! Well, they never did run very big to the barrel, but—ouch!—I agree!"

So he sat down and drew up the document. But Dan'l Webster kept his hand on his coat collar all the time.

"And, now, may I go?" said the stranger, quite humble, when Dan'l'd seen the document was in proper and legal form.

"Go?" said Dan'l, giving him another shake. "I'm still trying to figure out what I'll do with you. For you've settled the costs of the case, but you haven't settled with me. I think I'll take you back to Marshfield," he said, kind of reflective. "I've got a ram there named Goliath that can butt through an iron door. I'd kind of like to turn you loose in his field and see what he'd do."

Well, with that the stranger began to beg and to plead. And he begged and he pled so humble that finally Dan'l, who was naturally kind-hearted, agreed to let him go. The stranger seemed terribly grateful for that and said, just to show they were friends, he'd tell Dan'l's fortune before leaving. So Dan'l agreed to that, though he didn't take much stock in fortune-tellers ordinarily.

But, naturally, the stranger was a little different. Well, he pried and he peered at the lines in Dan'l's hands. And he told him one thing and another that was quite remarkable. But they were all in the past.

"Yes, all that's true, and it happened," said Dan'l Webster. "But what's to come in the future?"

The stranger grinned, kind of happily, and shook his head. "The future's not as you think it," he said. "It's dark. You have a great ambition, Mr. Webster."

"I have," said Dan'l firmly, for everybody knew he wanted to be president.

"It seems almost within your grasp," said the stranger, "but you will not attain it. Lesser men will be made president and you will be passed over."

"And, if I am, I'll still be Daniel Webster," said Dan'l. "Say on."

"You have two strong sons," said the stranger, shaking his head. "You look to found a line. But each will die in war and neither reach greatness."

"Live or die, they are still my sons," said Dan'l Webster. "Say on."

"You have made great speeches," said the stranger. "You will make more."

"Ah," said Dan'l Webster.

"But the last great speech you make will turn many of your own against you," said the stranger. "They will call you Ichabod; they will call you by other names. Even in New England some will say you have turned your coat and sold your country, and their voices will be loud against you till you die."

"So it is an honest speech, it does not matter what men say," said Dan'l Webster. Then he looked at the stranger and their glances locked.

"One question," he said. "I have fought for the Union all my life. Will I see that fight won against those who would tear it apart?"

"Not while you live," said the stranger, grimly, "but it will be won. And after you are dead, there are thousands who will fight for your cause, because of words that you spoke."

"Why, then, you long-barreled, slab-sided, lantern-jawed, fortune-telling note shaver!" said Dan'l Webster, with a great roar of laughter, "be off with you to your own place before I put my mark on you! For, by the thirteen original colonies, I'd go to the Pit itself to save the Union!"

And with that he drew back his foot for a kick that would have stunned a horse. It was only the tip of his shoe that caught the stranger, but he went flying out the door with his collecting box under his arm.

"And now," said Dan'l Webster, seeing Jabez Stone beginning to rouse from his swoon, "let's see what's left in the jug, for it's dry work talking all night. I hope there's pie for breakfast, Neighbor Stone."

But they say that whenever the devil comes near Marshfield, even now, he gives it a wide berth. And he hasn't been seen in the state of New Hampshire from that day to this. I'm not talking about Massachusetts or Vermont.

The Cobra's Hood

By RUPERT SARGENT HOLLAND

*Wherein a priest of Bengal takes an amazing
revenge on the thieves of his temple's ruby.*

I

How this ice make grow in your country? Him
grow on tree? Him grow on shrub?" asked a learned
and elegant Parsee of Captain Littlefield in the bazaar
of Calcutta. The captain punctiliously explained that
the ice was frozen water from Wenham Lake, Massachusetts, in the United States of America.

"Frozen water, my dear sir!" said the Parsee, with
all the graces of an Anglo-Indian civil servant. "But
him would melt when the sun is hot!"

"Yes, indeed," agreed the American skipper. "But
Mr. Frederick Tudor's ship *Tuscany,* in which I
brought the cargo to Calcutta, is double-sheathed on
purpose to protect the ice from melting, and we pack
it in pine sawdust as an insulator."

This story is from Yankee Ships in Pirate Waters *by Rupert Sargent
Holland*

Eben Bowditch, the supercargo, left the captain explaining to the Parsee and went on to the offices of
Jamsetjee Jeejeebhoy & Company to dicker for return
freight for the *Tuscany*. To ship ice to India was, he
appreciated, an idea worthy of a Napoleon. Friends
had laughed at Mr. Tudor when he mentioned his
scheme, and told him it was idiotic; but the Boston
merchant had sent out the ship that spring of 1833 with
one hundred and eighty tons of ice, and Captain Littlefield had landed almost two-thirds of the cargo in good
order on the banks of the Hoogly.

The Anglo-Indian community in Calcutta was de-
lighted with the novelty and immediately regaled itself
with long iced drinks, which helped to make the hot
and sultry climate supportable to those of foreign birth.
Englishmen learned to mix their drinks Yankee-fash-
ion, and in gratitude played host to the officers of American ships lying in the harbor. Eben Bowditch, young
and adventurous, and tasting India for the first time,
enjoyed to the full the parties in the houses of English
residents and at their clubs.

To such a party he proceeded when he had finished
his business with Jamsetjee Jeejeebhoy & Company. He
dined with Major Arbuthnot of his Britannic Majes-
ty's Indian Army, and later sat in a garden looking out
on the Hoogly, where the guests smoked expensive
cheroots and tinkled no less expensive ice in their tall
glasses. It was late when he made his adieux, and taking his gold-headed malacca cane—a recent and highly

prized purchase—from the Major's turbaned body-servant, stepped out into the lane that would bring him to the harbor front where his ship was moored.

The lane led him first to an open square, and he had no more than come into this when he found himself spectator of some sort of midnight scuffle. In the square stood a Hindu temple and down the steps of this building a crowd of angry natives, with loud cries and threats, were hustling a couple of men in European dress.

The latter were being soundly pummeled and as the natives continued the belaboring after the two white men had been thrust from the steps Eben Bowditch felt his anger rise, and gripping the malacca stick tightly in his fingers, he sailed into the press of bobbing turbans.

He laid about vigorously with the stick, so vigorously that he was able to win clear through to the white men, who were now retreating before the belligerent natives. A Hindu struck at him with his fist, and Eben parried the blow with his up-thrown elbow. He whirled the malacca cane above his assailant's turban, but before he could bring it down a stout cudgel caught the American a clip over the head that stretched him on the ground.

When he opened his eyes he was not in the square and there were no angry chocolate-skinned men trying to get at him. He felt no surprise at that, for he had forgotten all about the melee into which he had so impetuously thrust himself; all he was conscious of was that his head ached abominably. Presently, however, the aching eased sufficiently for him to gather his wits enough to look about him, though he felt little curiosity as to what had happened. He saw that he was lying in the bottom of a boat, his head pillowed on some rough sacking. He put his hand to his head and felt a bandage bound tightly about his temples.

The exertion made his head throb again and he lay still for some time. Gradually his interest roused and his senses became clearer. The sky above was not so dark; the deep purple was changing to saffron along the horizon. Trees and bushes were moving, trooping to right and left; he heard the ripple of water—evidently the boat in which he lay was floating or being propelled along some stream.

He put out his hand to the gunwale, thinking to rise; but the effort made his shoulder sting as if seared by a hot iron.

"Take it easy, matey," said a voice. "Lie where you are. You got a crack on the head would've felled a rhinoceros."

Eben Bowditch lay back, lay quiescent for a space while dawn took possession of the over-arching sky and showed him the figure of a man in white duck trousers and blue jacket who, squatting in the bow, rhythmically raised and dipped a paddle. He heard another paddle churn the water behind him; there were then two men in the boat. Now he remembered something of what had happened; he had got mixed up in a fight in a square of Calcutta; two white men had been set upon by a lot of natives—probably these two in the boat were those men.

"Something knocked me out, did it?" he asked presently. "Struck me on the head?"

"It certainly did, young feller," said the man in the stern of the boat. "Down you went, easy as you please. And then the Hindus, thinkin' you was done for, took to their heels and disappeared so fast you couldn't see 'em go."

"What started the rumpus?" the American asked after some minutes of reflection.

The stern-paddler chuckled. "Bill Bates an' me wanted to have a look at the inside o' the temple—we'd heard there was jewels in there, a lot of idols decked out in gems—but the priests got mad when we pushed in, and first thing we knew the Hindus were pushing us out. A rum set of coves those Hindu priests, acting so rude to a couple of nice-behavin' an' sedate-like British tars."

Another pause; then Eben Bowditch said: "So you picked me up and took me to your boat and bandaged my head? That was mighty decent of you."

"Couldn't leave you there, bleedin' like a stuck pig," said Bill Bates from the bow. "You're a Yankee, ain't you?"

"Yes, I'm from Boston. Eben Bowditch is my name, and I'm supercargo on the *Tuscany*."

"That's the ship that brought the cargo of ice?" said Bill Bates.

"Yes. And I wish I had some of that ice on my head now. Gee! but it would feel good."

"We'll give you a pannikin of coffee by an' by," said the man in the stern. "My name's Tom Larkins; bosun on the British brig *Latona* of Hull."

Eben Bowditch glanced at the forests moving along the shore. "Where are we? Where are we going? Out to your ship?"

"Not this morning, Mr. Bowditch," said Tom Larkins. "We're going up the Hoogly. Current's running well; we must be all of ten miles above Calcutta by now."

"But why do you want to go up the Hoogly?" Eben Bowditch asked, feeling much mystified. "Did your captain send you up-stream to trade with the natives?"

"Not exactly. No, the captain didn't," Larkins answered in an amused tone. "You might call it a private trading trip. Bill an' I have a bit o' business to do on our own. Maybe you can fill your pockets too at the same time."

The supercargo pondered this while he watched the sunlight splash the trees and vines with brilliant gold. Why, he wondered, were these two English sailors going up the Hoogly into the back country of Bengal? Why had they not turned him over to some of the American seamen on the water-front at Calcutta to transport to his own ship? The whole affair seemed curious to him. However, the *Tuscany* would not sail for a week—perhaps not for a fortnight—his head was not throbbing so much now, the warm sun was very pleasant; it was more agreeable to watch the trees and doze than to think.

The boat pushed its nose into sedges along the river shore and Bill Bates, splashing in the water, pulled it up on the bank. "Feel like a bite o' breakfast?" Tom Larkins said to Eben Bowditch. "We've brought along plenty o' grub, bacon an' coffee an' a couple o' tins of hardtack."

Eben Bowditch felt surprisingly hungry and when the other two had helped him out of the boat and he was seated in the shade of a tall bamboo, his back resting against the ribbed bole, he watched with great satisfaction the building of the little fire, the bubbling of coffee, the sizzling of bacon.

The two British tars looked to Eben like the usual run of sailors, hard-fisted, somewhat truculent-featured; but they obviously meant to be friendly and supplied him plentifully with food and drink. Then they lighted stubby clay pipes, and when Tom Larkins had got his tobacco going he cocked an eye at Eben.

"Beginning to feel more like yourself?" Larkins questioned. "I always heard say that you Yankees were hard-headed, and now you've proved it. Still feel a bit groggy, eh? Well, I don't wonder with that crack on the head; but you'll be right as snuff in a day or two." He nodded in friendly fashion.

"I reckon I will," grinned Eben. "But how far are you two going up the Hoogly?"

"A matter of a day's paddle, accordin' to what we heard in Calcutta." Larkins smoked for some minutes in silence. "You see this is how it is. This bloomin' country is full of temples, an' the temples is full of heathen idols, an' the idols is plastered all over with rubies an' emeralds an' the Lord knows what else."

"Sinful shame, I call it," vouchsafed Bill Bates. "Keepin' things like that locked up in temples where they cawn't do no good."

"So it is," agreed Larkins fervently. "Think what we—or any white men—could do with the bloomin' jewels! Take a couple of 'em, say—nice, big emeralds or rubies—an' we wouldn't have to work no more."

The other sailor was looking at Eben Bowditch over the bowl of his pipe. "See what we're gettin' at? We was plannin' to take a view of the idols in that temple at Calcutta—see how the jewels was strung on and so forth—when they shoved us out an' along comes you."

Eben Bowditch was beginning to understand the motive of his companions.

"Well, I should think you found out very promptly that the priests and the people didn't want any strangers poking around their temples. Even I—with my wits knocked galley-west—can see that."

"That's right, they don't," agreed Tom Larkins. "But there's richer temples in India than them in Calcutta,

197

an' some of 'em are in places where there ain't many people, two or three priests maybe guarding the idols in what they call a shrine."

"We heard about 'em in Calcutta," went on Bill Bates. "A handful of priests to a temple, maybe not so many. We was thinking that half-a-dozen men from the *Latona* could handle a temple proper, but when we put it to some of our pals they said they didn't think they'd care to go along. Then you happened in, and Tom says to me: 'Here's a likely cove; takes to a fight like he enjoyed it. We're all ready to start, but we need another hand; let's take him along; he's a regular fire-eater.' That looked pretty good to me; three's better than two when it comes to a scrap."

"I could see you was a gentleman," added Larkins, "an' I thought maybe that would help in gettin' us into the temple."

Eben Bowditch tried to loosen the bandage on his head, which was throbbing vilely again. These two men who had picked him up in the square were low-down thieves, their thoughts centered on despoiling some Hindu shrine of its jewels. He felt chagrined, insulted, at the brazen impudence of them in thinking that he would help them in their robbery, share their spoils or steal loot on his own account. But his aching head forbade his expressing his indignation or even remonstrating with them; he would have to wait a later opportunity.

Larkins was speaking. "We've heard that up the

Hoogly there's a temple with a wonderful ruby they call the Cobra's Hood—"

Eben Bowditch didn't listen to any more. He was wishing for a lump of cold Wenham ice to hold at the back of his neck.

II

Sometimes the boat paddled by Larkins and Bates met a square-sailed Indian barge carrying market produce down the river to Calcutta, sometimes it passed a village, built of mud and thatch and sticks, where women were washing clothes on a floating platform in the water. There were fields of rice, cotton, and lentils; there were stretches of thick, impassable jungle; there were swamps in which crocodiles splashed and above which squawked noisy, raucous parrots. The two Englishmen kept steadily to their labor during the heat of the day; Eben Bowditch, his head throbbing with the hot glare of the sun, lay in the bottom of the boat, one arm crooked above his aching eyes.

They did not stop for a midday meal; Larkins and Bates munched hardtack where they sat and quenched their thirst from a water-bottle. Eben drank some water, but had no stomach for food. On they went again until the sun commenced to descend and the river to cool; then the boatmen paddled their craft to shore and invited the American to share their supper.

The cooler air and a tin of coffee helped to clear

Eben's head and he began to consider his two companions with a more lively interest. The two appeared to
him to have become more secretive or more circum-
spect; they talked less freely and said nothing more of
their business up the Hoogly.

Probably, Eben Bowditch thought, Larkins and
Bates felt that he did not approve of them and therefore now regarded him as an encumbrance rather than
as a helper in their enterprise. They were civil to him,
but nothing more. Occasionally he caught them ex-
changing glances that seemed significant to him of their
new feeling and when they packed up their cooking-
kit at the edge of the water he observed that they whispered and nodded to each other.

Well, he certainly did not approve of them if they
intended to try to steal jewels from native shrines, and
if they had reached that conclusion without any hard
words between them it was so much the better for them
and him. They might hail some down-river barge and
put him aboard it. The sooner he saw the last of them
the more he would be pleased. He was comfortable here
on the soft grass, much more comfortable than he had
been on the boat; stretching out full length, he pillowed
his head on his arm and fell into a light doze.

The chattering of crows, flying inland from the river
to roost, wakened him and for several drowsy minutes
he watched them wing away. His head felt very stiff
and he had to make an effort to lift it and another to
sit up. Everything was quiet about him. He looked at

the river, now smooth as glass; there was no boat visible on it, apparently he had the place entirely to himself.

Tom Larkins and Bill Bates had vanished, taken French leave. Eben Bowditch frowned; that was not the way white men should treat a fellow who had been wounded, and wounded in an effort to help them. They had cast him off with as little concern as if he had been an old boot for which they had no further use. They had not even left him a tin of hardtack nor a bottle of water. Evidently they didn't care at all what happened to him and would without any compunction have marooned him on a desert island.

This cold-blooded betrayal made him mad and he got to his feet so quickly that it started the throbbing again. But in spite of the pain he was intent on action. He looked up and down the river, but saw no boat of any kind. In the morning he might sight a boat; he would not stay here until morning, however; he would try to get to some native village along the Hoogly.

The ground was cleared for some distance up the river and he started off in that direction. He felt weak —his legs as well as his head ached with the exertion —but he stumbled on until he came to tall grasses that were so thickly enmeshed he couldn't push through them. He slumped down by a bush and half-closed his eyes in sheer weariness. Then he heard a slithering noise, so unique and somehow so uncanny that he quickly looked around. What he saw sent icy fingers running up and down his spine.

An immense cobra was swaying within a couple of arm-lengths of him. The snake was nearly eight feet long and gave the impression of standing up. Most of its length was a gray-white, but on the hood that spread out like a gigantic bulb were spectacle-marks of a mottled color that in the dusk appeared to be reddish-brown. The cobra's eyes glinted like rubies, and eyes and hood, moving slowly, were the most utterly fearsome objects Eben Bowditch had ever seen.

Eben drew back. He had nothing to strike with. He seemed to have lost the power of motion. He stared at the swaying serpent, which appeared to him to grow larger as he stared. He knew the reputation of the extraordinary-looking reptile; he had heard much of India's poisonous snakes in Calcutta; how fatal was the venom in the cobra's fangs. And this was a monstrous cobra; what the natives called a King Cobra; indeed a monarch of its tribe.

The snake was swaying nearer; its tongue was darting in and out. Eben tried to summon his will power, tried to move farther back into the bush. Then from somewhere floated a voice, the voice of a man speaking soft, low words. There were gentle footpads, and a hand touched the American on the shoulder. The voice continued; and now the cobra turned its swaying head and hood and proceeded with undulating motion toward the jungle grasses.

Eben, who had been tense as a taut bowstring, relaxed with a sigh of relief. He was shivering, his hands were clammy, his face was beaded with perspiration. He made an effort to get to his feet, and it seemed as though the fingers that touched his shoulder were helping him to rise. He stood up and found himself gazing at a tall and very emaciated figure, a man with wrinkled brown skin and long straggling hair, clad in a single cotton garment that reached from neck to knees. This man said something in a soft tone that was scarcely above a whisper. Eben Bowditch did not understand the speaker's words; all his attention was focused on the man's luminous and compelling eyes.

Eben had never seen such eyes; he felt that they were looking at him and through him at the same time. Wisdom was in them and power, an impersonal force shone from their depths. Eben knew that the stranger was a holy man, a priest of some sort, and understood that it was by his will that the cobra, instead of striking, had taken itself off to the jungle. The stranger's eyes were drawing him, and obedient to their will, Eben followed and walked without any feeling of pain or even fatigue.

They came presently to an open space that was like a dim green bowl set in the midst of darker green woods and thickets. On the farther side rose a stone building that from its conformation Eben took to be a temple. There was also a low house of thatch and to this the guide led the American and on the threshold gestured for the latter to enter. Eben went in and sat down upon a couch covered with a magnificent striped tiger skin.

Very strange were the sensations of the young super-cargo from Boston; he felt as though he were living in a dream and had no longer the power to direct his own thought and motions. His wounded head might have accounted in part for that feeling, but it seemed principally due to the strange influence that emanated from the Hindu priest. There was no need of commerce in words between that man and Eben; the Hindu's eyes perfectly conveyed the message he wished the other to receive.

Eben rested on the couch and the priest removed the hard, blood-caked bandage that bound his head. Gently massaging Eben's scalp with fingers dipped in a sweet-smelling oil, the other murmured words in a crooning voice. Under the voice and the fingers the American became drowsy, his heavy-lidded eyelids dropped; when he opened them again all the pain and throbbing were gone from his temples, he felt as though he woke from a sleep that had restored his strength.

The Hindu placed before his guest a bowl of rice and lentils, a cup of fresh water, and when the latter had eaten and drunk his host led him to the door and out to a moss-covered log that was set like a bench against a row of trees. The night sky was lighted with stars, the air was cool and refreshing. The two sat together and the harmony of that quiet place filled Eben Bowditch with perfect satisfaction.

He felt that this infinitely wise man knew all about him; about his home in Boston, his voyage in the *Tus-*

cany, his coming up the river with Larkins and Bates. He felt that the man had sensed his peril from the cobra and had purposely come to his rescue. There was nothing, it seemed to Eben Bowditch, that this extraordinary personality would be unable to do. For a time they sat there, filled with the peace and quiet, then rose as by a single impulse, and went again into the house. Eben slept like a babe; in the morning he was as vigorous as he had ever been.

All sense of strangeness or surprise had passed from him. The Hindu priest went to the temple and came back to where Eben was lazing in the sun. The priest's eyes spoke to Eben and the American understood: something had been stolen from the temple; from Eben's memory floated the words of Tom Larkins— "We've heard that up the Hoogly there's a temple with a wonderful ruby they call the Cobra's Hood—"

III

There was a river village north of the temple and thither the Hindu and the American went after they had eaten their noon meal. The priest appeared to be in no haste and spent considerable time in talking with the natives; he was, Eben inferred, seeking information concerning any strangers who might have been seen in the neighborhood. The whole matter was clear to Eben Bowditch; Larkins and Bates had located the ruby they wanted and had probably stolen it during the night;

they would now be on their way back to Calcutta with their very valuable prize.

That evening a barge drew up at the village and the priest with punctilious politeness indicated that Eben was to go aboard with him. The Hindu showed neither concern at his loss nor eagerness to be in pursuit of the robbers; he sat on the deck, contemplating the water and the shores with the calm, philosophic detachment of the carved figures of his majestic gods.

They reached Calcutta the next day. Eben pointed out to the Hindu the *Tuscany* at anchor in the harbor and indicated that it was his ship. The priest bowed, his lips smiled; and then each went his way, but Eben had the firm conviction that they would meet again.

Captain Littlefield was very much pleased to see his supercargo, as nothing had been heard of that young man since he had walked out of Major Arbuthnot's house several evenings before. He listened to Eben's story of the fracas in the square, of the rescuers who turned out to be jewel thieves, of the cobra and the priest. "The fellow did you a good turn," the captain declared; "those hooded snakes are deadly poisonous. I've heard of how some of the natives are able to charm them, but I've never seen the trick done myself. And he mended your head? Aye, I see he did; you look as good as new."

"I've never met a man like that Hindu priest, Captain Littlefield," Eben said. "He gives you the feeling that he has the most tremendous, mysterious power, and

unting-room of the Calcutta shipping firm
Captain Littlefield, Kalan Dass, the dig-
of the Company, and the clerk with whom
vious day Eben had discussed the Cobra's
n Dass waved Eben to a chair and Captain
promptly explained the business that en-

offered an exceptionally favorable price on
said he; "a very considerable discount on
eady arranged, if we will clear the *Tuscany*
tta by sundown today and sail for Singa-

ade all arrangements," stated Kalan Dass,
may leave at once. There will be no dif-

reason why we shouldn't sail," said Eben
My bills of lading and accounts are all in

reason either," agreed Captain Littlefield.
r hand I see a very good reason why we
ill mean a very neat increase to the profits
e." He glanced at Eben and the latter
etected a slight wink in the captain's eye.
ondition attached: that we should take a
te priest as far as Singapore."

hun Mai will not wish to go with you as
ore," said Kalan Dass; "he may decide to
f the islands. But he would sail with you
oday." The Indian merchant's black eyes

yet he seems so simple, so like a thoughtful child.
It's amazing—" He broke off, realizing that it would
be impossible to explain the priest's effect on him
to so practical-minded a man as this Yankee shipmaster.

"Well, I'm sorry those two rascals got away with his
ruby," said Littlefield. "They were the thieves, of
course; no native would think of stealing from a temple. But the priests ought to keep better guard over
their shrines; it don't do to put too much temptation
before foreigners. Once they get away with the loot,
as these two did, it's as good as gone; the priests can't
prove it on them and while they're trying to, the thieves
sail off for other ports."

That sounded like common sense, and yet as Eben
Bowditch thought the matter over he had the profound
conviction that Larkins and Bates would not succeed in
keeping the ruby and that the gem would presently be
restored to its rightful place in the temple.

Business took him the next day to the offices of Jamsetjee Jeejeebhoy & Company and with a very polite
Indian clerk, who spoke excellent English, he discussed
cargoes and prices relevant to the *Tuscany's* return
voyage to Boston. This business concluded, Eben inquired: "Have you ever heard of a temple jewel that's
called the Cobra's Hood, a ruby of great size and
beauty?"

The clerk smiled in the slow and thoughtful fashion
of his people.

"Oh, yes, Mr. Bowditch, sir. Everyone in Calcutta, everyone in Bengal, has heard of that jewel that reposes on the breast of a goddess in a temple up the Hoogly River."

"It's a queer name to give a jewel that belongs to a goddess," Eben suggested.

"The Cobra's Hood?" mused the clerk, as though the idea that the name might be considered strange had never occurred to him. "Ah, but the cobra is by way of being considered sacred in Bengal, Mr. Bowditch. And near that temple there are said to be many cobras that have the jewel under their protection. Have you ever seen a cobra, Mr. Bowditch?"

"Once," answered Eben. And, feeling a sudden distaste for pursuing the subject, he hastily picked up his papers and left the shipping clerk.

Sugar, coffee and cotton made up the *Tuscany's* cargo out from Calcutta and for a week Eben was busy checking consignments of these as they were put aboard the ship. Occasionally he wondered what the Hindu priest was doing to regain the ruby, but as he neither saw the man nor heard of him he concluded that his curiosity would have to go unsatisfied.

Then one day as he waited on the water-front for the longboat he saw a brig that flew the British flag set sail down the harbor. There were English sailors loafing on the shore and Eben accosted a couple of them.

"What's the name of yon ship?" he said; "the brig there outward bound?"

"The *Latona*," said ⋯
Singapore."

Eben's curiosity w⋯
the crew?" he asked. "⋯
Bill Bates aboard he⋯

The sailor nodded. ⋯
well. Those two blo⋯
are aboard the brig. ⋯
off with my own eye⋯

"Rascals, eh?" sa⋯
call them that?"

"Well, it's only a ⋯
Britisher. "Larkins ⋯
Tom; prime Yorks⋯

"They didn't get ⋯
Eben asked casuall⋯

"Not that I kno⋯
would've come off⋯

So the thieves ⋯
taken the ruby wi⋯
that they must hav⋯
molested in the p⋯
with their loot? ⋯
Hindu's affair an⋯

As he stood th⋯
whom he recogn⋯
Jeejeebhoy & C⋯
Company's offic⋯
in English. "Th⋯

In the c⋯
Eben foun⋯
nified head⋯
on the pre⋯
Hood. Kal⋯
Littlefield ⋯
gaged then⋯

"We are ⋯
our cargo," ⋯
the terms al⋯
from Calcu⋯
pore."

"I have n⋯
"so that yo⋯
ficulties."

"I see no ⋯
Bowditch. "⋯
order."

"I see no ⋯
"On the oth⋯
should, as it ⋯
of the voya⋯
thought he ⋯

"There is a ⋯
very high ca⋯

"Perhaps ⋯
far as Singap⋯
land on one ⋯
by sundown ⋯

fastened on Eben's face. "This priest is a man of very remarkable wisdom and power; there is no one in Bengal more highly regarded than Chun Mai."

Eben looked at the clerk. The latter was softly smiling and the American understood that he was thinking of their talk concerning the Cobra's Hood. It was strange, Eben reflected, how in India thoughts appeared to be so much more potent than words.

"Well, we'll take the priest and we'll sail this afternoon," said Captain Littlefield, his forthright voice breaking in on the spell that seemed to have settled on the room. "Tell Chun Mai to be on the wharf at three o'clock and I'll have a boat waiting for him."

Outside, as they walked to the harbor, the Yankee shipmaster chuckled. "I reckon I can see through a pane of glass as well as anyone, Mr. Bowditch. This priest is the one who rescued you from the cobra and healed your head, the big 'medicine man' as our American Indians say. And of course he's after the ruby those Britishers stole from his temple."

"Yes, sir," said Eben. "And the two thieves sailed on the *Latona* this morning for Singapore. They must have the jewel with them or Chun Mai wouldn't be sailing with us. But what I can't understand is why he didn't take it from them here in Calcutta; I should think that would have been a simple matter for a man so influential as Chun Mai seems to be."

"Ah, but they don't do things out here in India as we do at home," said the captain sagely. "Perhaps he didn't want to kick up a row in this town where the English are important. They move more slowly here; time doesn't count for much with them. But I'll bet a handful of good Yankee dollars that Chun Mai has got it all thought out and that he'll get the ruby from the thieves if he has to travel all the way to England after it."

That was Eben Bowditch's thought likewise, and he very much wanted to see how this wise and powerful priest of the temple was going to deal with the thieves.

IV

Chun Mai came aboard the *Tuscany* that afternoon and was greeted by the master and the supercargo. Eben showed the Hindu to a stateroom that had been set apart for him. This was, Eben supposed, the first time that the priest had ever been aboard a vessel of the type of Mr. Tudor's ship, but so far as he could see Chun Mai was in no wise impressed by the novelty of his surroundings.

From her anchorage the *Tuscany* moved down the river to the mouth of the Hoogly and into the broad waters of the Bay of Bengal. Soon after leaving Calcutta Chun Mai seated himself cross-legged in the bow. He was a strange figure in his coarse white cotton garment and straw sandals, and the Yankee sailors eyed him with a good deal of curiosity, considerable amusement, and not a little awe.

Eben brought the priest a bowl of rice and a cup of water at sunset; Chun Mai accepted these, ate and drank and returned the empty utensils with a smile of thanks but no words. Stars shone in the sky, an orange moon rose and gilded the shores of India. Men aboard the ship went about their occupations, but the priest of the temple sat without stirring, as aloof from the life around him as the figurehead that adorned the *Tuscany's* bow.

Eben wondered next morning when he went on deck if Chun Mai had sat there all night; the priest was in the same position, his eyes contemplating the dawn light on the sea. Strange, thought Eben, that a man could so completely cut himself off from the outside world, wrap himself so absolutely in a mantle of his own occult philosophy. The American shrugged; the ways of these Oriental worshippers were a mystery to his Western mind.

Presently he brought food to Chun Mai and the priest broke his fast and again thanked Eben simply with a smile.

The *Tuscany,* favored by the wind, sailed smartly through the Bay of Bengal on a southeast course that would bring her between the northernmost of the Andaman Islands and the coast of Burma.

For a day and another night the voyage was without incident. The crew had by now lost all curiosity concerning the Hindu, regarding him as simply part of the deck furniture as much to be taken for granted as windlass or mast. Captain Littlefield and Eben discussed him occasionally. "I reckon he'll go as far as Singapore with us," observed the captain. "He don't show any signs of wanting to leave the ship."

The second day, after noon, some of the small islands were sighted that lie in a chain north from Sumatra toward the tip of Burma. Eben watched the specks enlarge into stretches of yellow sand and green-crested palms. Then his eyes caught the glint of sun on a sail flitting southward. He turned to look at Chun Mai. The Hindu was still gazing with level eyes at the glittering floor of the sea.

Within half an hour the weather had changed most astonishingly. Eben Bowditch, unused to the Indian Ocean, watched the transformation with rapidly mounting interest that soon quickened to excitement. Veils of cloud obscured the sun and the horizon commenced to glow like beaten copper. The air, which had been cool, became warm, then hot and hotter. The sea, which had been translucent blue, became an oily, muddy greenish-brown.

Captain Littlefield came from the after-deck and stood, hands clasped behind his back, looking out at the olive-colored water, the specks of islands, and that other ship, now plainly visible from waterline to masthead. Once he turned toward Eben, and the supercargo thought the master was about to address him, but instead the captain pulled a bandanna handkerchief from a pocket and mopped his perspiring brow.

A trance appeared to have fallen upon the *Tuscany* and her crew. No order was given to take in sail or change the vessel's course. The sailors stood about the decks, watching the copper band widen on the horizon, as if the rim of a metal pot were drawing in around the ocean.

Lightning quivered in a circle low down in the sky. The air was now sultry, oppressive; Eben Bowditch felt himself bathed in a heavy sweat. To take a step forward would be burdensome; he grasped a ratline in his fingers and looked at the back of Chun Mai's head, at the bowsprit just above it, and at the other ship that made a line with these.

The trance-like period lengthened while the two ships moved in a hot wind over the oily floor of the sea toward the islands that were now a purple-black against the copper horizon. Eben had the sensation that both vessels were being drawn by a magnet, that they were no longer wind-propelled, no longer directed by the helmsman at the wheel. Some occult power was hovering in the path between the islands. As he felt this, he saw the look of sky and sea suddenly change. A bank of cloud rose from the water and was joined by another bank from above. These two, now one, commenced to revolve rapidly, in appearance something like an hourglass, narrow in the middle and flaring above and below.

A waterspout was bearing directly on the other ship and whirling faster and faster. It changed form, elongated, assumed fantastic shapes; its colors shifted, ran the gamut of the rainbow, seemed actually to shed light from themselves.

Eben, staring ahead, saw Chun Mai rise, saw his long emaciated arm steal out from its sleeve, saw the fingers point above the *Tuscany's* bowsprit. Eben looked where those fingers directed, at the other ship and the portent in the sky. The waterspout was dissolving, coalescing again; and now it swam up into the arch of heaven like a gigantic serpent, rising in coils from a broad base.

The portent widened, swelled near the top. The serpent had a hood, milky white for a moment, then veined with blue and purple, then violet changed to red. Now it shone like a ruby, with a fire of its own; it was a great eye of rose—

Eben Bowditch broke the spell that bound him. "The Cobra's Hood!" he gasped.

Chun Mai let his arm descend.

Those aboard the *Tuscany* saw that other ship caught by the waterspout and twisted and wrenched like a toy in the hands of a giant. The ship was flung up and down, disappeared in the cloud that swallowed it in its maw, was seen again in fragments, masts snapped off, canvas shredded to ribbons, rudderless, a mass of timbers and little else.

V

Captain Littlefield abruptly became voluble. "That wrecked ship's the *Latona,* of course!" he called out to Eben Bowditch.

"So I suppose," said the supercargo, still looking at that whirlpool of water and column of cloud that had shown such a remarkable resemblance to a hooded cobra.

"Rum thing!" said the captain and strode to Chun Mai who, at the sound of footsteps, turned and quietly smiled.

The crew of the *Tuscany* were moving now, as if released from some spell. Eben let go his hold on the ratline and walked over to the rail.

The waterspout was circling away to the southwest, beyond the line of islands; the mass of it was dissolving, unwinding from a spiral, trailing off in dun-colored clouds that were like drifting smoke.

A cooler wind crossed the water and freshened the Yankee crew. The copper band on the horizon changed to primrose yellow as the sun again swam into view. Ocean and sky were quiet again. But there in the passage between two of the islands floated the hull of the wreck and some of the ship's company were in the water, clinging to scattered spars.

"Stand ready to lower the boats," ordered Captain Littlefield, as the *Tuscany* bore down on the battered brig. "We'll pick up the crew."

"The Cobra's Hood!" gasped Eben . . .

But others were before the Yankees in that work. From the islands on either side proas had swiftly darted and brown-skinned men were hauling the white sailors into their boats.

"Malays," said Captain Littlefield, "and pirates most likely. Well, they'll hand over those men to us or I'll know the reason why!"

Chun Mai touched the captain's sleeve and pointed to the proas and then to the nearest island.

"What do you think he means?" the captain murmured to Eben Bowditch.

"I think he means that he will deal with the Malays and would like to be set ashore," hazarded the supercargo.

"Shall I do that?" said Captain Littlefield. "You don't think he'll set the islanders to murdering the brig's crew?"

Eben Bowditch smiled. He remembered the evening he had spent with the priest under the stars, the quiet and refreshment that had seemed to emanate from the holy man. "Chun Mai is a man of peace," he answered. "He has come to get the ruby that was stolen from the temple. He would harm no innocent man, of that I am sure."

"But how about the two thieves? They're rascals, of course, but I don't want—" the captain hesitated.

"What Chun Mai wished to do, he will find the way to do," Eben responded.

"Eh? What's that? Yes, yes, you're right, quite right,

Mr. Bowditch. That waterspout—looked like a snake
. . . Queerest thing I ever saw on any of my voyages."
The captain nodded to the Hindu and said, "I'll have
a boat put you ashore."

The second officer commanded the longboat that was
rowed to the island nearest to the *Tuscany*. Eben Bowditch, with the captain's permission, made one of the
landing party, while the *Tuscany's* master stood ready
to fire his guns or come to the rescue in the ship's
boat at first sign of hostility on the part of the
natives.

The brown-skinned men at close view looked utter
savages to the supercargo; some were armed with
kreeses, some with spears, and the shining eyes in the
dark faces were ruthless and vengeful. Eben thought of
the stories he had heard of Malay pirates and their
treatment of white mariners shipwrecked on their
shores. Men such as these would delight in slaying those
they pulled from the sea.

They had brought ashore the men from the brig and
the English sailors, half-drowned, were lying on the
sand and in the long grasses. The Malays were eyeing
the men in the longboat with suspicion, with malevo-
lence. The bow grated on the shingle and Chun Mai
stepped over the side. Somberly the islanders stared as
the Hindu walked up through the water and came into
their midst.

They drew back for him and the priest went on to the

English sailors, those sprawling, battered, water-sodden men. Eben saw Chun Mai halt, look at the recumbent figures, then go forward and stoop over one. The long fingers tore away the shirt from the man's chest and a moment afterward Chun Mai was holding aloft a leather bag from which dangled a broken cord.

From this pouch he drew its contents, and even at that distance Eben Bowditch could see the sun strike light from the magnificent ruby in the priest's hands. Once Chun Mai raised it, then he pocketed it again. Turning to the islanders, he said something to them, and the brown-skinned men, like obedient children, drew away to the palms above the shore.

Chun Mai came down to the longboat and looked at Eben Bowditch. As clearly as by spoken words the American read the message that shone from those deep, compelling eyes; the priest had accomplished his mission, he would take the jewel back to the temple in his own way; peace and serenity he sent with his friend to his home across the sea.

"He means to stay here, doesn't he?" said the second officer of the *Tuscany* as he watched the tall figure of the Hindu move toward the interior of the island. "I don't understand what it's all about, but I reckon it's none o' my business. He's a queer one, and I can't say as how I'm sorry to have him leave the ship. But he's certainly fixed things up for us with those Malays; I don't think they'll trouble us now."

"I don't think they will," agreed Eben Bowditch, and wading ashore he went over to the English crew. The one with bared breast was Tom Larkins, the bosun, who had apparently been knocked unconscious in the wrecking of the brig. Near him lay Bill Bates, and that rascally tar, catching sight of Eben, lifted himself on an elbow. "Holy cripes!" he grunted. "I seen him take it from Tom there, and I'm mighty glad the blame thing's gone!"

The men from the *Latona* were taken aboard the *Tuscany*. The English ship was too much damaged for salvage, so Captain Littlefield set sail that evening for Singapore. The master and the supercargo, standing at the rail together, saw a proa with lateen sail steal out from behind a headland of the island and scud away to the north. "There he goes," chuckled the captain. "Chun Mai's commandeered a Malay skiff, same as he did this ship of Mr. Tudor's, and he's carrying that precious Cobra's Hood back to its home on the Hoogly. It's a small boat for such a trip, but"—the captain laughed loudly—"I'll bet my pay it won't run into any bad weather on the voyage to Calcutta, let alone meet a waterspout."

Eben Bowditch smiled. "I won't take your bet, sir. The man's a wonder."

"Mighty neat trick," said the captain. "He didn't raise any row with the English in Calcutta. It just happened that the *Latona* fell in with a waterspout, same as any ship might. Only you and I have our little suspicions and they aren't such as most folks would take any stock in."

"Larkins and Bates do," declared the supercargo. "I've been talking with them and they both swear it was a cobra—of gigantic size—that struck their ship."

"All sailors yarn about sea serpents," grinned the captain.

"Well, I don't know," said Eben Bowditch. "That waterspout was the spitting image of the hooded cobra I saw in the bush, the one that did Chun Mai's bidding. All I can say is that that Hindu priest has got some power we white men can't begin to understand."

"That's so," agreed Captain Littlefield. "And I reckon we'll have to leave it at that. But don't you go telling this yarn to your folks in Boston or they'll think you've got a touch o' the sun."